Courting Captain Nemo

Mad Scientists Society

Book 3

To all my niblings: May you live a life full of new discoveries and surrounded by good friends, good family, and good (Polish and Indian) food!

Special thanks to Farisa for her help with Nisha's heritage and the Bangla language. Captain Nemo shines all the brighter because of you!

For notes on content please visit

catsteinbooks.com/content-notes

Courting Captain Nemo

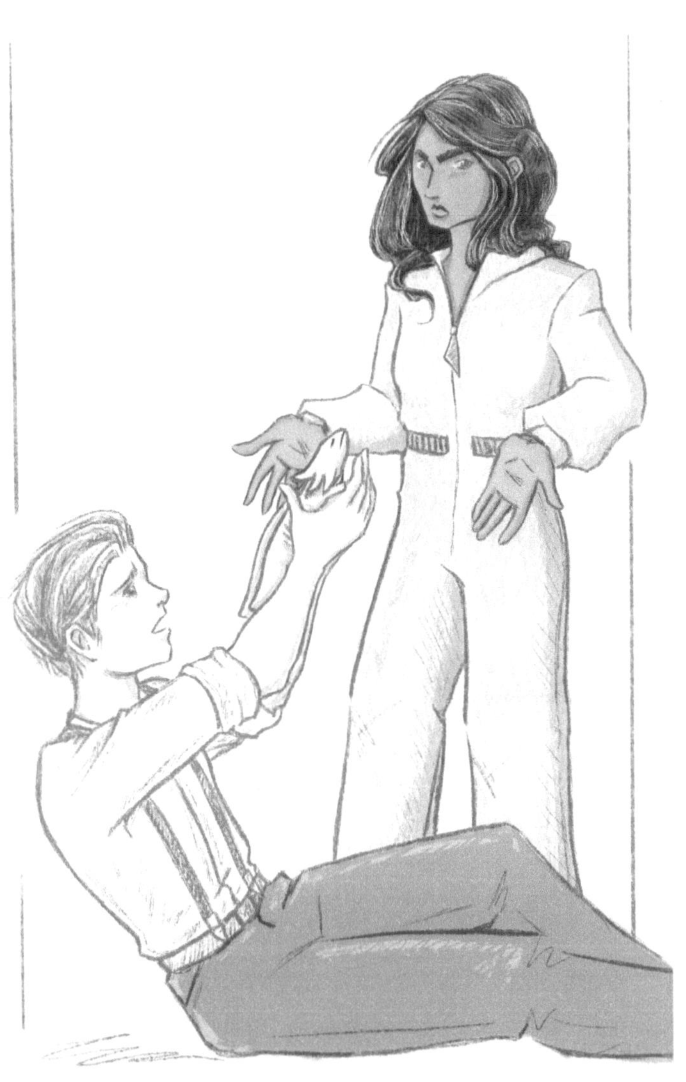

"Water!"

Chapter 1

Captain's Log, 19 June, 1892
All systems in working order. Weather fair. Voyage to proceed as scheduled.

Aleksy Szekalski hadn't considered the possibility of mortal peril when he'd decided to steal an axolotl. He hadn't considered much of anything, really, beyond the poor creature's welfare. Impulsive, Mama would say. *Mój drogi, you must think before you act.*

He never learned.

Heavy footsteps pounded on the pavement behind him. Too near. He was losing ground.

Don't look back. Don't look back.

The brutes chasing him were bigger, stronger, faster. And armed with wicked, double-edged knives. Even a glance could cost him his life. The axolotl wriggled in his hands. Already her slimy skin had begun to dry. If he didn't get her into water soon, she'd die. His rash decision might have doomed them both.

Aleksy veered around a corner, heading for the river. Even on a Sunday, people would be at the docks, wouldn't they? Please, please let there be people. His pursuers couldn't kill him in front of witnesses.

His legs burned as he raced through the shipyard,

dodging and leaping equipment. Behind him, the men cursed and shouted.

Too close, too close.

In the distance, a cluster of people stood along the riverbank, peering out at something in the water. Could he reach them in time? Would they hear if he called out?

Aleksy's chest ached with every gasped breath. Sweat poured down his face, running into his eyes and obscuring his vision. He had to make it to the water. He had to. He would not let this poor, abused animal die. He would not let those villains get away with their nefarious deeds.

Muscles shaking, he ran on, aiming for the long dock near the group of people. All he needed was to leap off it into the river. The axolotl would be safe. The men couldn't harm him in public. Everyone might think him mad, but he had no social standing to lose.

"Stop, thief!" one of his pursuers shouted.

Blast. Now the people on the dock would think he was the criminal. Which, technically, maybe he was.

"Help!" he shouted, though his heaving breaths made the word half a gasp. "Help! They want to hurt me!"

Heads turned in his direction. Between his panting and his thick accent, could they even understand him?

"Stop them!" he cried.

His own footsteps pounded in his ears as he finally reached the wooden planks jutting out into the river. One jump and he'd be in the water. The animal would be safe. Then he could pause and consider his next move.

The dock creaked beneath him. He readied himself to leap. One step more and—

Aleksy flailed, trying to stop his forward momentum. Before him, where open water should have been, lay a smooth metal surface, punctuated by a single round hole.

He pitched forward, stumbled, and fell, cradling the axolotl to his chest to protect it from harm.

His backside hit the metal hard, sending a jolt of pain up his spine. Instinctively, he thrust out a hand to steady himself, but the hand landed on nothing but air, and he tumbled through the hole, down into darkness.

He didn't even have time to scream. He crashed to a stop, the blow knocking all the air from his lungs. Above him, the hole began to close, cutting off his only source of light.

He couldn't breathe. He couldn't breathe and the world was going dark and he'd failed. The axolotl flopped lethargically in his arms. She was dying. He'd failed her.

Aleksy fought to draw in a shaky breath. Overhead, the hole closed with a definitive clank.

In the same instant, electric lights snapped on all around him. He lay on the floor inside some enormous metal machine. All above him were pipes and tubes. Beneath him hard steel. Footsteps sounded, echoing in the hollow space.

A face appeared, and a pair of beautiful dark eyes glared down at him. "What the hell are you doing on my ship?" the woman demanded.

Aleksy held up the axolotl. "Water," he gasped.

* * *

Well, this was an inauspicious beginning to her voyage. Nemo frowned down at her unexpected passenger. Where had he come from? The dock had been clear of people when she'd boarded the ship and started the descent sequence. She couldn't have been below for more than two minutes.

"Water," the stranger repeated. "Please."

Nemo eyed the animal in his hands. An amphibious creature, she guessed, seven or eight inches in length, with mottled tan and olive skin, a round belly, and a wide head crowned with odd feathery appendages. It flopped in the man's hands, as if in distress.

"Ah. Your animal needs water."

That was a simple problem. This room, the main living space of her submarine, included a fully stocked kitchen, as well as a table for recreation or dining. Nemo strode the few steps to the sink.

"Hot or cold?" she asked.

The man struggled to his feet, wincing. "Cooler than the air. Not cold." He had a thick accent. Eastern European of some sort? Here in Detroit, one heard so many accents and languages, it was difficult to keep track.

Nemo opened one of the many cabinets in the wall and selected a large bowl. She placed it in the sink and turned the spigot. Cool water, filtered directly from the lake, poured into the bowl. The man rushed over, tested the temperature with a finger, then plunged his animal into the water. When the bowl was filled, he carried it to the table. The creature swam slow circles in the small space, already looking perkier than moments before.

"What happened to its arm?" Nemo wondered. The animal was missing half its front right limb.

The man scowled and bit off a harsh retort in a language she didn't understand. Nemo jumped. Potential nearby weapons flashed through her head.

The stranger steadied himself with a deep breath. "I am sorry if I frightened you. I am very angry." He gestured at the animal. "An evil man cut off her hand. It will grow back, but his cruelty is not forgivable. I stole her to save her from further harm."

Nemo's muscles unclenched. If this man made a habit of rescuing animals in need, he wasn't likely to mean her any harm. Which was good, since she'd be stuck with him for the next week. Better not to have to knock him unconscious and tie him up.

"What sort of animal is she?" Nemo asked. "I've never seen anything like her."

"*Ambystoma mexicanum*, a salamander of Mexico. Called 'axolotl' by the locals." He pronounced the names slowly to ensure she understood him.

"Axolotl," she repeated. "Pretty. She's interesting. What are the feathers on her head? Decoration, or do they serve a purpose?" This wasn't how Nemo had expected to acquire her very first specimen, but already her brain had jumped to explorer mode, wanting to gather as much data as possible for her notes.

"Gills," the man replied. "She can also absorb air through her skin and she has lungs and will sometimes surface to capture bubbles of air."

"You're quite knowledgeable. Are you a biologist?"

A sad expression filled his eyes. "I have no official university degree."

But some sort of unofficial one? Curious.

A flash of red light and a beeping noise made her head jerk in the direction of her control room. "Please excuse me. I need to return to the helm."

She shouldn't have stayed away so long. She'd set the submarine on a course, but the shallow, narrow river with its booming shipping business presented many possible obstacles. If she crashed and failed so soon after departure, she'd be a laughingstock. Captain Nemo would be no man's jest.

Her passenger followed her through the hatch. "We are sailing?" he asked. "Where? For how long? I must return—"

Nemo ignored his gasp of surprise. She'd spent enough

time here on the bridge that it was nothing but ordinary to her. Her fingers ran across the numerous switches and dials of the wide control panel, silencing the proximity alarm. Through the large, semi-circular panel of windows, she could see the riverbed spread out before her. Even in the slightly murky water, she could discern the shape of a sunken steam car. She flipped a few switches and turned the main rudder, steering to avoid the obstacle.

"Is that a motorcar?" her flabbergasted passenger wondered.

"A smuggler, most likely," Nemo surmised. "They were very active on the ice this past winter."

"Yes. I read in the papers." He stepped up beside her. "Where are you going? May we please stop soon? I must return home."

"I'm afraid I can't stop," Nemo replied. She stepped to her left, to the panel with the ship's interior controls. If he became enraged, she would shut off the lights and run for a weapon. He'd be left flailing in the dark and easy to incapacitate.

He turned to look at her. "I… Pardon?"

"I won't be stopping," Nemo explained. Not for seven days. No matter what this intruder wanted. She wouldn't give up her life's work for him or anyone. "It's impossible. You're here for a week. You'll have to make do."

She glanced over at him. His jaw had gone slack, his blue-gray eyes wide with horror. Keeping all empathy from her voice, she gestured at the hatch and said, "Please return to the living quarters, sir. Food is available in the galley, and bunks and a washroom are further aft. Welcome aboard the *Narwhal*."

Chapter 2

Captain's Log, 19 June, 1892
Have acquired unexpected passengers. 1) human male, 25-30
years of age, unhappy but non-hostile, name and origins as
yet unknown. 2) axolotl female, injured but healing, 8 inches
long, age unknown.

This wasn't happening. How could this be happening? Aleksy's idea had been simple: sneak into his employer's office, steal the axolotl, run. On a Sunday morning, he was the only person in the building, he'd thought.

Then he'd been chased by secret security guards, and now he was trapped inside this extraordinary underwater boat with a woman who might possibly be evil.

No, she couldn't be evil. She'd been kind and helpful about the axolotl, and seemed genuinely interested in the animal's welfare. But to insist he remain here for a week? Why? Why not find a reasonable place to stop and let him out?

Unless she was a prisoner too?

"Is there another person on this boat?" he asked softly. His gaze darted around the room, wondering if someone might be listening.

The room was a marvel. Windows as tall as a man covered the entire curved side of the semicircular space.

Below these stood a huge array of levers, gauges, wheels, and other controls with purposes he couldn't begin to understand. A sturdy chair sat before what appeared to be the main steering wheel. To both his left and his right were additional chairs, large and plush, like in a library, and behind him, running from floor to ceiling, was an entire wall of books.

Aleksy struggled not to turn around for a better look. He wanted to peruse each and every shelf, touch the leather spines. He wanted to know what volumes made up the library of this strange craft.

It's not important. You need to get off this boat.

The strange woman glanced away from her controls, assessing him with those fathomless dark brown eyes. "Someone else on board?" she asked. "Only if you brought them with you."

Aleksy took a step toward her, slowly. He'd already frightened her once and didn't want to do so again. He couldn't deny that it would be unsettling to have an unknown person appear on one's submarine vessel. As unsettling as it would be to accidentally fall onto such a craft.

"We are in the same boat," he remarked, grinning at his play on the English idiom.

"Indeed," she replied. "We shall make the best of it."

He nodded. "But not for a week. I must return home. When we reach a convenient location?"

"I'm sorry," she replied. "It's impossible. We will be in Lake St. Clair in approximately half an hour, and then we can talk more. Please make yourself comfortable in the meantime." She turned back to the controls.

Aleksy gazed out the windows. The long, pointed snout of the boat could easily snag on underwater debris, especially in a river full of smugglers' cars and... were those cannons? Yes, five or six of them in a jumbled pile off to the right of the boat. Old weapons, from the look of them. Which made sense. Detroit had been a French fort, once, later conquered by the British. He'd read all about the history of the city when he'd first arrived here, eager to embrace his new home. Only to discover no one else seemed interested. In fact, more than one person had called him a "dull bookworm."

Since his captor would likely also be bored by the history of Detroit or his opinions on the harm humans were doing to the river's flora and fauna, it was best not to remain in her presence. He would check on the axolotl and leave the woman to her task.

Aleksy turned and ducked through the hatch to the kitchen area. When they were in open water, he would talk to her again and plead his case. Surely she didn't want him here with her. He sank down onto one of the padded benches flanking the table and waited.

Good to her word, she stepped out of the control room very close to half an hour later, taking a seat across the table from him. She didn't speak immediately, and Aleksy allowed himself a moment to study her.

She was close to his own age, at best guess. Pretty. Her dark eyes were framed with long lashes. Long black hair had been tied back into a neat tail. Her warm, medium-brown skin appeared free of cosmetics, and her only jewelry was a pair of small diamond studs in her ears. Her clothing, too, was simple and plain, consisting of a one-piece coverall garment in rugged green cloth. Odd, for a woman, but practical. She'd attired herself for work aboard the boat, it seemed.

"How is your axolotl?" she asked, before the silence could become too awkward.

"Well, I believe. I doubt she is happy with the small space, but she appears unharmed by her adventure."

The woman nodded. "I have specimen tanks large enough for her in storage. We can fill one up. And if you need to add sand, salts, minerals, or anything of that sort, I have some available, or we can take a sample from the lake bottom. But first, we must discuss your presence on my ship. Who are you and why are you here?"

"My name is Aleksy Szekalski, and I am here because I fell." Did she really think his appearance here was anything but accidental? As if he would trap himself here by choice? "I rescued the axolotl and was taking her to water. I didn't see your boat until it was too late. I slipped and fell into it. I would like to return home as soon as possible."

"A week," she said again.

Aleksy sighed. "I'm sorry, Miss—"

"Captain," she corrected. "My name is Nisha Majhi. My friends call me Nemo. You may call me Captain."

"Majhi. I have heard that name."

"Most people have. My father is chief of police."

A shiver coursed through Aleksy. Police. Would they be after him if he returned to the city? Technically, he had stolen the animal. Taken her right out of his employer's office. Which meant he also didn't have a job anymore. Not that he'd enjoyed sweeping floors. But it had paid the bills.

"Will you turn me in for stealing the axolotl?" he asked. "Is that why you are keeping me here? You tell me a week so I am unprepared when you stop and hand me over?"

Her eyebrows shot up. "Of course not! I am *not* a liar, Mr. Szekalski, and would never call the police on someone for attempting to help a fellow creature. When I say a week it's only because we must remain underwater for a full seven days."

Aleksy rested both elbows on the table and put his head in his hands. "I do not understand this. It is not…" He groped for the English word. The more upset he grew, the harder it was not to slip back into his native Polish. "Not logical."

"This submarine is on an extended test voyage," Miss Majhi—*Captain* Majhi—explained. "I have a patron willing to fund my research expeditions. We will be able to explore the Great Lakes as never before. Ultimately, the *Narwhal* can be taken to the oceans. These are unexplored territories. Places of new and exciting discoveries waiting to happen. Advancements in our scientific understanding of the world!"

A worthy purpose, Aleksy had to agree. An expedition to study the flora and fauna of the seas would be a dream come true. The type of dream he could never hope to achieve until he could obtain a university degree. No one would take him seriously without credentials.

"The only way this patron will provide the funds is if the ship passes a rigorous array of tests," the captain continued. "I will be keeping records of her speed, depth achieved, ease of maneuverability, seaworthiness, onboard comfort, and ability to remain submerged. She is not only to set the record for longest time underwater, but to shatter it. A full week is the price of the bargain. If I surface before then, for any reason, the test will be forfeit and I will lose my chance to achieve scientific progress. I'm sorry you found yourself in the middle of it, but it's only a week."

Aleksy lifted his chin slightly to look at her. "Is there no other way? No other patrons?"

Her mouth compressed into a thin line, but when she finally replied, it was with the same cool tone she had used before. "No other patrons are willing to sponsor a woman engineer with an outlandish ship."

"I'm sorry." And he genuinely was. Clearly this woman

was brilliant, to have created this marvel of a boat. And yet too many would ignore her because she didn't fit their narrow idea of what a scientist ought to be. Things were the same the world over.

He dropped his head back into his hands. What could he do? His options were terrible. He could continue to insist she release him, knowing it would be the ruin of her dreams. Or he could surrender and accept the consequences of a week here with her.

He jerked upright. There would be consequences. Many of them. He didn't even know if he could live here. She hadn't been prepared for him.

"How can I stay here?" he blurted. "I have no food. No clothing. And we are all alone. What will people think when they discover where I have been? What will they say? We will have to marry."

Miss Majhi rocked back in her seat, eyes going wide. "I beg your pardon!"

"It's true. Already I have been alone with you too long. To be here with you a week… You will be… What is the word? Destroyed?"

Her surprise faded. "Ruined? No. I'm already too peculiar. I wear trousers. I'm an engineer. I drink whiskey and go to the club with my male friends. I'm already unlady-like and unmarriageable. You're safe."

Aleksy shook his head. She was far from unmarriageable, no matter how peculiar she might be. Who wouldn't want a beautiful and clever wife?

"But you?" he asked. "If I ruin you, will your patron take away the money?" He was going to crush her dreams, no matter what he did. He was a walking disaster.

Aleksy reached out a hand toward the bowl where the

axolotl rested. She lifted her head to peer at him. At least he had done one thing good today.

Captain Majhi considered his words a moment. "I think we can handle the situation. When the week is up, I will drop you off wherever you like. I can choose a spot where you won't have to worry about anyone seeing you. Then you won't need to fear the police, and I won't have to explain your presence. As for living here for a week, you'll have no trouble. I have enough stores of food for a month, and I have several boiler suits like the one I'm wearing that should fit you." She waved a hand at her utilitarian clothing.

"The food might be trouble," he admitted. He cringed and glanced away from her. She would think him strange. Ridiculous. "I…" He steeled himself for her laughter or mockery. "I don't eat meat."

"You're a vegetarian?" If she was surprised, she hid it well. "That's no problem. I have plenty of meatless options. My family hails from Bengal, and vegetarians are not unusual in that part of the world. Also, my uncle married into a Muslim family, and they have their own dietary restrictions. Adjusting to personal food preferences is nothing out of the ordinary. I hope that eases your worries?"

"Tak. Yes." Apparently she had a sensible answer for everything. Which meant this was really happening. He was about to spend the next week on an underwater boat with a woman he'd just met.

This dull bookworm was going on an adventure.

Chapter 3

Captain's Log, 19 June, 1892
Shallow water tests complete. All systems operational.
Course set for Lake Huron.

The sink in the tiny washroom hissed and popped, spitting water in erratic bursts. Aleksy sprang back, then scrambled to turn the tap off. How had he managed to break something *already*?

The captain should have told him no touching, period. Instead, she'd given him free rein throughout most of the ship. She'd only warned him not to touch anything in the engine room.

Aleksy glanced at the toilet beside the sink. Eventually, he would need to use that. Hopefully he wouldn't break it too.

He stepped out of the washroom and peeked into the shower next to it. Back home, he would have said it looked nice. It sported separate hot and cold knobs for adjusting the temperature, and a well-spaced array of jets would allow for efficient washing of one's entire body. Much quicker and easier than a bath.

Except that he was on a submersible boat and apparently here he couldn't even work a sink. Worse, every time he washed, or even changed clothes, he'd be naked in close proximity to a woman who was very much his superior on this ship and almost certainly well above him in social standing. It would be awkward at best, and potentially could get her ostracized, whatever she said about her reputation.

He walked back to the small bunk room that was to be his home for the next seven days. Three identical bunks jutted from the wall, with barely enough space beside them for a man to stand. Storage cabinets lined the walls at either end of the room. He'd found bedding in the drawer beneath the bottom bunk and made up the middle bunk for himself. The unadorned sheets were crisp, with a freshly cleaned scent. Overall, it was an austere living space, but not dreadfully uncomfortable.

Down on the floor, the axolotl swam about happily in her new enclosure. It would be nicer once he could get some sand for the bottom of the tank, and perhaps some large rocks or sticks she could hide behind. But for now, it was enough that she was safe from harm. The next step would be to find her something to eat.

He strode to the front of the ship to find the captain tapping a pencil against a clipboard that held an extremely long checklist. Most of the items had been marked off, and several had numbers or words jotted beside the entries. She consulted a dial on her control panel, wrote something on the paper, and then checked off one more item.

"Can I help you?" she asked, her eyes still on the list.

"Do you have any worms?"

She looked up sharply. "Worms?"

"I need to feed Nadia."

Her brow furrowed. "Nadia?"

"The axolotl. I named her Nadia because it means hope."

"Ah. That's appropriate. No, I don't have any worms at the moment. But we can scoop up some soil from the lakebed, if you'd like. That should get you some worms or snails, and perhaps some small fish. I can show you how to operate the sampling arm as soon as I finish with the shallow water tests." She waved her list.

"May I look?"

"Of course."

She handed him the clipboard and he scanned the paper. She'd been right to call her tests "rigorous." The list contained a whole host of things he would never have thought to report on. Temperature at front and back of the ship, both inside and out. Oxygen levels. Air circulation. Inside pressure. Outside pressure. Hull—

"Hull *deformation*?" he blurted. His gaze flew to the ceiling above him. "Is your ship not seaworthy? Are we about to be crushed?"

The captain snatched the list from his hand. "Not to worry. The *Narwhal* is designed with a certain amount of expansion and contraction of the materials in mind. We're not likely to see any noticeable change in that measurement unless we go quite deep or into water that is particularly hot or cold."

Aleksy couldn't look away from the ceiling. There was water up there. Above them. "What happens if something goes wrong?"

Something hard nudged his arm, and he looked back down. The captain held a metal liquor flask with an N engraved in the center.

"Have a drink," she suggested. She motioned to one of the leather armchairs. "Sit down and we'll talk."

Aleksy accepted the flask and sat. He unscrewed the cap and took a small drink. The alcohol had a smooth, rich, oaky flavor. The heat of it was pleasant in his throat, not scorching. Captain Majhi had good taste. He took another swig, counting on the alcohol to help ease his nerves.

The captain took the seat opposite him. "That whiskey comes from across the river in Windsor," she said. "Do you like it?"

"It's nice," he replied. "But not my favorite. When we return, I will get you some good Polish wódka. *That* is the best."

"Ah." She tilted her chin in a tiny nod. "I'd like that. Now, about the ship. I don't want to lie to you and tell you absolutely nothing could go wrong. Something can always go wrong. But what I will tell you is that I have prepared with that in mind. I spent years conducting small-scale tests before I even began to build this vessel. After that, I tested every component in turn, making certain they could do what I needed. The *Narwhal* has been built with the absolute highest quality parts, and anything I didn't build with my own hands I still checked over myself. She is as sound as I could make her, and I'm confident she will not fail.

"Even so, she is equipped to handle problems. You heard the proximity sensor earlier. She has other warning systems to tell us if we are in any danger. Should that happen, I would bring her to the surface at once. Our lives are far more valuable than finishing any test."

"And if she is disabled to the point that she cannot surface?" Aleksy asked.

"We would launch the Minersible."

Alesky shook his head. "I'm sorry, I don't know that word."

"Oh, I invented it. Short for miniature submersible. It's a tiny craft meant for closer inspection of anything we wish to explore outside the ship, but it can also be an escape in an emergency. So you see, we're quite safe."

"Thank you." He capped the flask and rose from the seat,

crossing the room to hand it back. "I will let you finish your list, unless there is anything I can do to help?"

"I don't think so. I have only a few required elements left. My patron wants daily speed tests, for instance. But it's silly to test speed here. With the shallow water and proximity to land, there simply isn't enough space to safely move at top speed. Only in completely open, deep water would we want to go that fast. I won't push her past nine knots today. But she theoretically could go at least twelve here. I suppose I'll just put nine and mark it done."

"If your patron is serious about your research, he will want to know the practical limits of the ship, not the theoretical limits," Aleksy said.

"Excellent point. And we'll be in Lake Huron for several days, and it's thousands of square miles in area and hundreds of feet deep. It will give me ample opportunity for testing." She marked off the speed on her list, checked a few more things, then removed the paper from the clipboard and stashed it in a narrow drawer beneath her control panel. She pulled a few levers and the submarine began to slow. "We can rest here safely while I show you a few things."

Aleksy followed the captain to the engine room at the rear—aft—of the boat. In terms of size it was the largest room on the ship, but the amount of machinery made the space as cramped as his tiny bunk room. A pair of six-foot-tall copper boilers flanked a closed rear hatch, generating the steam that powered the wheels of two large engines. The continual hiss of steam through the pipes filled his ears, punctuated now and then by the clank of a gear.

"Here."

Aleksy froze, hugging his arms across his chest so he wouldn't accidentally bump anything. The captain had stopped only two steps into the room. Beside her, along the starboard side of the ship, was a panel of switches and wheels that looked like a small version of the controls on the bridge.

"The sampling arm," she said. She flipped a switch. The floor beneath Aleksy's feet vibrated. "This starts up the machine. When the light here turns on, it means the arm has touched the bottom and is ready to scoop. Spin the dial for small, medium, or large scoop." A small light turned green. "Perfect. Would you like to do the honors?"

He hesitated a moment, then gingerly reached out for the button she indicated. The moment he pressed it, the vibration beneath his feet intensified. A low grinding sound rose up from the floor. Aleksy shivered, but the captain remained calm. A few moments later, the green light turned red and the vibrations halted.

"All done!" the captain announced. "Step aside, if you please."

He shuffled back and Captain Majhi knelt down to open a panel in the floor. Beneath them lay a metal box full of murky lake water, sand, and one small fish.

"Feel free to take whatever you like from the sample," she said. "You can find tools to scoop and carry in the galley. When you're done, flip the switch back to 'off' and the machine will dump any excess."

"Thank you." Nadia could eat that fish, even if the sample didn't contain any other creatures, and he could spread the sand on the bottom of her tank. Even if it made little difference to the axolotl, it would provide him with something to do.

"But before you begin, I have two things to show you." The captain gestured across the narrow aisle to another panel of instruments. "First, this is our wireless telegraph. It works best if we are stationary and near land. When we stop for the night, you can send a message to anyone back home who might wonder where you are. We need it to be short and simple, so take your time and think what you'd like to say."

A smile broke across Aleksy's face. A message! He didn't know Morse Code, but the captain probably did, and perhaps she also had a book in her library. He could send word to his mother to say he wasn't dead or in trouble.

His smile faded. Maybe he shouldn't mention trouble. He'd committed a crime, lost his job, and was in an enclosed vehicle with an unmarried woman. Not ideal.

"Thank you," he said to the captain. His problems could wait.

"You're welcome. Last, this is our periscope. It will allow you to look up above the water while we are submerged. Feel free to use it whenever you like, especially if you are feeling confined or in need of sunshine. I personally find watching the waves and the birds and the jumping fishes relaxing. It's simple to use. Lift it up and look through. It turns in a full circle. I should return to the helm. Let me know if you need anything further."

"Thank you," he said again.

He took a moment to look through the periscope. The day was sunny, with little wind to ripple the blue-green water. A few boats chugged by in the distance. One small steamboat, with a white hull and mauve trim, puttered not far behind the submarine.

Could it see them beneath the water? It didn't seem close enough to hit them, but he hurried back to the bridge to report it to the captain. As usual, she remained unperturbed.

With nothing else to do, Aleksy dug through the sample collected from the lakebed. He found a few worms to feed to Nadia and plenty of nice sand for her tank bottom. When he was satisfied that he'd given her the best enclosure within his limited means, he retired to the galley and found himself some cheese and an apple for an impromptu lunch. He wrote his telegram, edited it down to be as concise as possible, and when he'd exhausted that task, returned to the periscope.

The *Narwhal* moved smoothly along the river between Lake St. Clair and Lake Huron. Through the eyepiece, Aleksy could see the docks and buildings lining the water. A steady stream of fishing and shipping boats sailed past on their way to Detroit or Sarnia.

He turned the periscope to aft and jumped. That same mauve-trimmed boat was behind them, exactly as close as it had been before.

It's nothing, he told himself. *It's going the same direction we are. It will probably stop at Sarnia or Port Huron, or continue past us once we're in the open waters of the lake.*

He lowered the periscope and forced himself to return to the bridge to pick a book to read.

Hours later, after making a simple dinner of rice and beans and memorizing the alphabet in Morse Code, he checked the periscope one final time, to ease his mind. The captain had found a spot to drop anchor for the night, and the *Narwhal* rested calmly twenty feet beneath the surface.

Aleksy pushed the periscope up almost as high as it could go and took a look around. His heart sank. There, unmoving, was the same blasted boat as before. Someone was following them.

"Captain!" he shouted.

Chapter 4

Captain's Log, 20 June, 1892
Lake Huron exploration, day one. Speed and depth tests
successful.

"Captain!"

Not again. Nemo squeezed her eyes shut for a second, collecting herself. She couldn't entirely blame her accidental stowaway for his uncertainty. This was all new to him.

It was all new to her, honestly. No amount of practice could replicate the experience of a real voyage. She knew this ship inside and out, but there would always be more to learn.

She rolled her shoulders, trying to ease some of the tension from her muscles. Today would be her first real day of exploration. The first day of the rest of her life.

Nemo made a quick check of the sensors. No nearby obstacles. Good. She could spare a few seconds to chat with Mr. Szekalski. She jogged to the rear of the ship.

"The boat from last night, Captain," he said when she arrived. "Now that we are moving again, it's also moving. Do you want to see?"

"No. I believe you. I don't doubt they're following us. But I'm sure it's only my patron, checking that I'm abiding by the terms of our bargain. Once we dive deeper, they're likely to lose us."

"Good. I'm sorry. I will stop bothering you."

"It's not a bother. I'd rather have you alert and informing me of anything you find than ignoring something that concerns you. Anything else you'd like to tell me before I return to the bridge?"

"No. May I accompany you? I'd like to find another book to read."

"Of course." Nemo gave him a smile before she turned away. Thank goodness he was a reader. The *Narwhal* wasn't exactly a hotbed of entertainment.

She needed to do something with him. There had to be some task she could assign him to keep his mind and hands occupied. Then he'd have less time to worry about things like boats sent to supervise her. Keeping busy always worked for her. As long as there was something to do, she couldn't spare time for fretting.

"How would you like to be the ship's first crewman?" she asked.

He flinched. "Me?"

"Yes. You're here. And I could use an assistant from time to time. If I can delegate some tasks to you, I can concentrate more on our explorations." It was perfect. If he could take over some of her duties, she could spend more time with her maps and charts. And that would lead to discoveries. She would see things no man had seen before.

Mr. Szekalski gaped at her. "But I have no knowledge of boats or engineering. How could I be of service to you?"

His tone didn't suggest any kind of innuendo, but the idea jolted through Nemo's brain without prompting. He was a handsome man, after all, with a firm, square jaw, thick, dark hair, and eyes of an alluring blue-gray color. His lips were especially fine—plump, with an appealing curve. Those lips could serve her very well, indeed.

But he was a passenger and a near-stranger. Besides, she'd long ago sworn off such pursuits. They simply weren't worth the potential repercussions.

Back in her university days, she would have flirted. She'd been reckless then, and always an explorer. Until the day a young woman had been caught in a young man's dormitory room. The girl had been disgraced and forced to leave town. The boy had been reprimanded, but still graduated with honors. The whole thing made Nemo fume, even years later.

So, she'd become more discreet. And eventually stopped bothering. Her work was more important. She'd make a name for herself and prove to everyone that women deserved equal treatment and an equal place in society.

Starting with her new crewman.

Nisha eyed him up and down. The boiler suit she'd given him to wear had been tailored with her friend Victor in mind. But while Victor was tall and thin, Mr. Szekalski was of average height and stockier build. The coveralls stretched taut over his thick arms and legs, outlining the muscles beneath the fabric.

"You look strong enough to handle a bit of manual labor," she said.

He made a noise that wasn't quite a laugh. "Until yesterday, I was employed as a cleaning man. So, yes."

"Excellent. If you could cook meals, clean the kitchen, and sweep the floors, it would be a great help. Beyond that, some of the daily machine maintenance might be easier for a person taller and stronger than myself. And if you'd like to spend time here with me at the helm, I can begin teaching you the controls. They're not difficult to learn."

He considered a moment. "Thank you. I do prefer to earn my keep."

"Thank *you*, Mr. Szekalski."

And that was another thing. Addressing him by his surname felt much too formal. She didn't need him calling her Captain Majhi or Miss Majhi, either. Onboard ship she was Nemo. The scientist. The explorer. Nothing more, nothing less. He needed a similar moniker.

"You need an appropriate crew name."

He blinked at her. "What do you mean?"

"I'm Nemo. And you are…?"

"Nemo," he repeated. "Is that Latin? 'No man'? Because you're a woman?" He chuckled.

"And because I want to explore things that no man—no human—ever has."

He nodded. "I have no Latin name, but Aleksy comes from Greek, like your Alexander. It means 'protector.'"

The image of the little three-legged axolotl flashed through Nemo's mind. Yes. He was absolutely a protector.

"I can call you Aleksy, unless you prefer something else." She called all her friends by their first names. Establishing a friendly relationship with him would help the remaining six days pass smoothly. And hopefully fend off further inappropriate thoughts about his lips.

Nemo grabbed one of the reading chairs and dragged it beside her seat at the helm. "Here, sit. I'm going to take her down to ten fathoms, and then we can run today's speed test."

Aleksy sat, watching in silence as Nemo eased the *Narwhal* into a slow, steady descent. When the depth gauge hit ten, she leveled off and switched to the throttle to bring the submarine up to top speed. Today, they'd get a good sense of just how fast she could be beneath the surface.

Aleksy touched a finger to the depth gauge. "How much is a fathom?"

"Six feet."

"We are at sixty feet, then." He leaned toward the window. "Already the world is so different. The colors have changed. It's mostly blue now."

Nemo paused a moment to admire the lake before her. "It's lovely. Mysterious, in a way. She's equipped with various lights, when we do want a closer look at something. Or when we go deeper still and lose more sunlight. I hope to take her ten times as deep as this."

He let out a low whistle. "I would love to see that. We know so little about the animals that live in deep water. Maybe we could discover a new species!"

Their gazes met, and Nemo's heart thumped. Aleksy's eyes shone with excitement, and a broad grin lit up his face. He felt it. That thrill of possibility. That hunger to go further, see more.

Even Nemo's dearest friends had never quite grasped her desire for exploration. As much as she loved Hal and Victor, they were a different breed of scientist. They liked to lock themselves in their laboratories to work on their projects. To them, the outside world was a distraction. To Nemo, it was everything.

Now here she was, with a companion dropped in her lap by chance. And he seemed to have the same enthusiasm for scientific adventure that she did. Remarkable. Apparently, the gods were smiling on her.

She looked back to the controls to hide a silly grin of her own. "Let's see how fast this beauty can fly, shall we?"

For the next hour, she put the *Narwhal* through her paces, hitting a maximum speed of 12.7 knots, and a top sustained speed of 12.3. Aleksy hesitated to touch any of the controls, but was happy to hold the clipboard and write down anything Nemo reported. A reasonable beginning to their collaboration, she supposed.

She consulted her charts. They'd gone far enough. It was time for her first deep dive.

"I'm taking her down again. As close as we can get to the bottom. We'll have many things to record as we go, so have that pencil ready."

"Aye, aye, Captain." Aleksy smiled at her with the same eager expression as before. "Is that the correct response? I read it in a book about pirates."

"See, you do have nautical knowledge."

"Only from novels and one very long voyage across the Atlantic Ocean."

Nemo shrugged. "You've bested me there. I've never seen the ocean." Her gaze flickered across the gauges. "We're approaching fifteen fathoms. We'll make notes there and every five subsequent fathoms." One-by-one, she pointed out all the relevant sensors. "Pressure. Temperature. Air quality."

Aleksy jotted notes. He had neat handwriting. Better than hers. She might have to continue using him as her record keeper.

The depth meter ticked downward. Sixteen fathoms. Seventeen. Nemo's body began to vibrate. They'd passed one hundred feet below the surface. She was doing this. She was truly sailing to the depths of the Great Lakes.

Nineteen. Twenty.

"Performance check." Her voice came out with a slight waver. Damn. The captain wasn't supposed to show emotion. It was her job to maintain a level head at all times. Especially with a nervous crewman onboard.

Aleksy leaned closer to the controls. Closer to her. "Inside pressure?" he inquired, not sounding nervous in the least. Maybe she'd been right. Maybe giving him responsibilities distracted him from everything else.

"Holding steady," she reported. Everything looked good. Outside, the pressure was increasing and the temperature dropping, but the climate inside remained unchanged.

"Hull deformation?" Aleksy gave her a lopsided smile. Perhaps he was a little nervous after all.

"Zero. Continuing descent."

Twenty-one fathoms. Nemo's shoulders tightened. Based on her charts, they would be nearing the bottom soon.

Twenty-two. She focused on her sound-propagation indicator. Nothing near enough to trigger any lights on the display.

Twenty-three. Twenty-four. Twenty-five.

"Perfor—" Several lights flashed on to indicate an obstruction below. Nemo yanked on the controls to bring the descent to a halt. When the ship reached neutral buoyancy, she flipped the switch to shut off the interior lights, leaving nothing but the faint glow of a few small indicator bulbs.

Twenty-five fathoms. One hundred fifty feet. She stared out the window. As the water stirred up by the *Narwhal* began to still, the lake around her sharpened into view. Ahead and below them, the bottom of the lake spread out in an endless sandy landscape. Fish swam past, entirely uninterested in the now-motionless vessel. Light from above penetrated to some extent, but the entire world had become the monochrome of a photograph, only in blue.

"It's incredible," Aleksy breathed. His arm brushed hers as he pressed closer to the window. He murmured a word in his native tongue. "No one has ever seen this. No one has ever been here. Only us."

Nemo turned to look at him. Their eyes met and locked in the semidarkness. "The lake goes much deeper," she whispered.

His nod was slow, serious. "There's more."

Chills raced over her skin. "So much more."

His arm slid against hers as he leaned even closer. Nemo's breath caught in her throat.

"I want to see it all." The husky quality of his voice started a new wave of shivers oscillating through her body.

She pulled back abruptly. Never in her wildest dreams would she have imagined anything could be more seductive than the lure of the unknown. Discovery of the day: as enticing as exploration was, sharing it with a like-minded companion might be even better.

And potentially more dangerous. She couldn't let close proximity and shared passions lure her into irrational behavior. Of the members of the Mad Scientists Society, Nemo had always been the sensible one. It needed to stay that way.

She turned up the lights and pointed at the clipboard Aleksy clutched in his hand.

"Time for that performance check."

Chapter 5

Captain's Log, 21 June, 1892
Lake Huron exploration, day two. In deeper waters today.
How far can we go?

She had a microscope. In two days, Aleksy had gone from worried to excited to thanking God for the bizarre series of events that had put him here.

His fingers caressed the smooth brass of the instrument as he threaded a new slide into the viewing area. The last time he'd touched a microscope had been in Warsaw, five years ago. It had been old, and tended to fall easily out of focus, but he'd cherished it. Now he had a gorgeous, brand-new apparatus beneath his hands and a cup of lake water teeming with microscopic life. When he'd fallen off that dock, he'd tumbled straight into heaven.

Aleksy peered through the dual eyepieces, adjusting the focus to get a good look at the tiny crustacean in his sample droplet. A cyclopoid copepod, though he couldn't identify the particular genus or species. He lifted his head from the microscope and jotted a few notes in the notebook the captain had given him. A few more long looks at the animal, and he was able to sketch a basic picture of its features.

He poured the droplet from the slide back into the cup of lake water and pushed the microscope to the very center of the table, where it was least likely to accidentally fall off. He could examine this sample for hours, and would, if the captain didn't have other tasks for him today. But first, he wanted to peruse her library. In his brief glimpses, he'd seen a full shelf of atlases and geographic texts, another of nautical books, and a large section of general scientific reference. Surely among them were some books on the biology of the region. Hopefully with descriptions and pictures. If he was to give a good accounting of what organisms they'd encountered and where, it would help to have them more specifically identified.

Captain Nemo sat at the helm, the lights around her turned down low. "Hello," she called when he entered, not looking up from her work.

"Hello," Aleksy replied. "I wanted to ask if you had any biological identification books. To assist with my studies of our samples."

"Bottom shelves, port side," she replied. She touched something on the control panel and a pair of small lights directly above the bookshelves lit up.

Aleksy paused a moment before walking to the shelf. Remembering left from right had never been an automatic thing for him, and adding the nautical terms atop that only slowed his brain more. He located the correct shelf, scanned the titles, and selected a few that looked promising. Before leaving, he stepped up beside the captain. Outside the windows, the water appeared darker than he'd ever seen.

"How deep are we now?" he asked.

"Seventy-five fathoms."

He whistled. "And the numbers are good? It feels as comfortable inside as ever."

"Everything's perfect. She's humming along happily. I can't run a full speed test, though." The captain shut off all the interior lights and turned up the exterior lights, illuminating a wide swath of terrain ahead of them. "Look at this landscape."

Aleksy tilted toward the window for a better look, remembering at the last second not to put his hands down on the controls. Instead, he shoved his hands into the pockets of his coveralls and stepped closer until the edge of the console pressed against his thighs.

The lakebed here was no longer the relatively smooth plain of sand from yesterday. Instead, it undulated in mounds and valleys. The submarine cut smoothly through the water, like a train puffing past rolling hills.

"The entire area is like this," Nemo said. "Hills both small and miles wide. Some sloping gradually, others shearing off sharply. It's not a place to move quickly."

"Why would you want to? It's so beautiful. A place to linger, not to fly past."

Her head turned slightly and he caught the hint of a smile on her lips. He couldn't see more with the lights down, but he suspected her eyes were dancing. She played cool, the captain, but he'd caught unguarded moments yesterday when her excitement had shone through. There was more to her than the dispassionate mariner, though he doubted he would ever see beyond those tiny glimmers.

"I agree," she replied. "Proceeding slowly allows me to observe the terrain, compare it with my charts, and improve our understanding of the region. But I also need to remember that this is a test voyage, and if I don't properly report the ship's capabilities, I may lose some or all of my funding."

Aleksy sniffed. If her patron valued adherence to a strict testing format over proper recording of real-life conditions, he was a fool. And why did top speed matter in the first place? An underwater boat didn't need to outrun anyone.

"Today perhaps it's better to focus on depth than speed," he said. "We're going down more?"

"Yes." The captain checked her display of tiny lights. "We have room to descend further here. I hope to take her past one hundred fathoms."

Aleksy jiggled his leg, unable to bottle up the excitement bubbling inside him. One hundred fathoms? What would it be like so far down? What creatures would they find there? Already, he was imagining a comparison of the microbes at different depths. It could fill a whole book, if he were thorough enough. If he could write the foundational text on the microscopic life of the Great Lakes, people would have to take him seriously, even if his schooling had been informal.

He watched the gauge tick lower. Eighty-five fathoms. Ninety. Today, the captain wasn't stopping to record, but descending quickly. When they passed one hundred—six hundred feet below the surface—he sucked in a sharp breath. His gaze darted to the indicator of the hull deformation. Still zero. This ship was as solid as anything he'd seen.

Captain Nemo halted the descent. Off to their left, the ground rose sharply, almost cliff-like. A similar rocky formation appeared to the right, barely visible at the far reaches of the ship's lights.

"I'm going to take us slowly through this canyon," the captain declared. "It's quite deep here, and the ground looks to slope deeper still up ahead. I want to take us as far down as I can."

"Please." Aleksy's pulse beat a little faster. He wanted to touch the deepest point in the lake. If it were possible, he would swim into the water and feel the sand in his fingers, the cold on his skin. Touching the bottom through this machine would be as close as he could get.

"How can you tell how close we are?" he wondered. He couldn't judge the distance well here. Were those cliffs in the distance tens of yards away? Or hundreds?

The captain pointed at the long cone jutting from the ship's prow. "The *Narwhal*'s tusk. It's an echo-locator. It sends out and records pulses of sound. The longer it takes the sound to get back to us, the further away the obstacle. It's very sensitive at close range, but good generally for nearly a full nautical mile."

Ah. And her array of lights displayed where this detector sensed anything. Clever.

"And it tells us we can go deeper. Let's do that. Can we touch the bottom?"

"Here? No. The ground is too uneven. I don't want to risk getting stuck, or causing damage to the ship or the environment."

"Of course."

She must have heard disappointment in his tone, because she turned to face him. "But we could do it in the Minersible."

"Yes, please." It occurred to him a moment later that he had no idea what this "miniature submersible" might be. She'd never given any details about it, and she hadn't shown him. Was it dangerous? Was it even big enough for two people? Whatever it was, he'd take it, because he wanted to get as close to the lakebed as possible.

Captain Nemo slowed the ship to a crawl, easing her deeper as the ground sloped to the bottom of the canyon. With each fathom down, the number on the dial ticked up. The captain spoke not a word and barely moved, her entire concentration on the controls in front of her. Aleksy's palms began to sweat.

The ship came to a halt just shy of one hundred twenty fathoms.

"I'm dropping anchor here," the captain declared. "Less than fifty feet to the very bottom. Perhaps as little as twenty. We'll cover the rest in the Minersible." She turned on the interior lights and rose from her seat. "Follow me."

She led him all the way through the ship, to the back of the engine room, where a hatch sealed off whatever lay on the opposite side. The captain tugged on a heavy steel lever, and the hatch creaked open. She pushed it wide and stepped through. Aleksy climbed after her.

Her miniature submersible took up almost the entire space in the small chamber. Aleksy squeezed around it, considering it from all sides. A sphere made of glass panels set into an iron framework comprised the bulk of the vehicle. The ball stood near to five-feet in diameter, and was held several inches off the floor by four squat legs. Fins and a propeller sprouted from a steel box attached at the rear. In the center of the box, an access hatch similar to the door to this chamber allowed passengers in and out.

Nemo opened the hatch and gestured for Aleksy to enter first. He poked his head in. A single bench seat stretched across the center of the bubble. Pedals and handlebars like on a bicycle allowed for steering. He crawled in and seated himself in the center of the bench.

"This craft is meant for one," he said, though the captain obviously knew this already.

She squeezed in beside him. "We fit. You can pilot her, since touching bottom was your idea."

We fit. Barely. The glass was so thick his head had only a few inches of clearance. If he moved to either side, he'd need to lean. And he couldn't pedal and steer unless he sat in the center. He shifted to give Nemo as much space as possible.

No good. The entire length of her thigh pressed against his. Their shoulders rubbed together. A faint floral scent wafted from her hair.

He cursed under his breath. This was a working relationship. He shouldn't be sniffing her hair. He *absolutely* shouldn't be touching her. But in the cramped quarters of the Minersible, what choice did he have?

Nemo reached past the handlebars and twisted a knob on the small control panel. A *thunk* vibrated up through the seat, followed a moment later by a faint rushing sound.

"Sit tight," the captain said. "Once the chamber is full, the ramp will lower and we'll slide out."

"Full?" The answer came before the word was entirely out of his mouth. All around the bubble, water flooded the room, rising inch-by-inch. His head snapped around to glance over his shoulder.

"Don't worry. All the hatches are fully sealed. The release mechanism won't function if they're not."

Aleksy turned forward again and nodded. He scooted over once more, trying to put space between their bodies. All the movement did was give her room to wriggle into a comfortable position. Wriggle against him.

Kurwa, he swore silently. Wasn't the thick fabric of the boiler suit supposed to afford better protection than this? He'd swear he could feel the heat of her body seeping into him.

Water. Think about the water. The cold, cold water.

Fortunately for his peace of mind, the water rose quickly, bubbling up around the sphere, first to eye level, then up over his head. He had to force himself to keep breathing normally. This was no different than the submarine.

The floor shifted beneath the Minersible, and it began to slide downward. A shiver of excitement raced from the top of his spine out to the ends of all his limbs. He was going down, to the dark, mysterious depths of the lake, separated from the unknown by only this tiny bubble of air.

"Pedal," the captain reminded him. "The handlebars will steer the rudder."

"Oh. Yes. Sorry. I got a bit excited."

"I could tell." Her gaze dropped momentarily to his jiggling leg.

Dammit. She could probably feel his every movement. How mortifying. He hoped she didn't think he was rubbing up against her on purpose.

Aleksy's occasional dalliances had always been with women of his own class. Casual acquaintances he could speak to bluntly. But Nemo was the captain. They had a professional relationship. They were, perhaps, even becoming friends. Now, here he was, not even knowing how to sit this close to her, let alone say anything.

Nemo reached past him to grasp a dial on the control panel, giving no sign that their proximity affected her in any way. Maybe she wasn't attracted to him. That would be a relief. His imagination wouldn't get carried away if he knew nothing could ever come of it.

"I'll control our descent," the captain told him. "You pedal and steer."

A pair of lights winked on the moment the craft popped fully free from the submarine. Aleksy threw himself into his role as pilot, allowing himself to revel in the adventure. Keep the excitement where it belonged. He pedaled in a smooth rhythm, propelling the Minersible through the dark waters toward a low spot a short distance ahead.

His heart began to pound. They were the only people ever to see this. The only ones ever to touch this deep. He steered resolutely toward that low spot, as Nemo inched the submersible lower.

The vehicle bumped as the feet touched down. Aleksy's legs froze, and his hands jerked away from the handlebars.

"Matko boska," he gasped.

"We're here." Nemo's words were soft, reverent. The exact opposite of his own blasphemy. She placed a hand to the glass. "We did it."

Aleksy splayed his palm on the glass beside hers. The thick window kept out the cold, but he imagined the feel of the water, icy and wet against his skin, and the soft sand squishing beneath his feet. A small, spiny fish darted past, either unaware of or unconcerned by the humans behind the glass.

"It's incredible," he breathed.

The fish turned around and swam past again. Perhaps it was curious about the submersible after all.

"It's magical," Nemo murmured. "Just think what we might discover here."

She glanced at Aleksy, and their eyes locked. Her warm exhalation caressed his face, stirring the stubbly hairs he'd been unable to shave over the past few days. Lord, she was so close. Kissably close. What had he been thinking, to lean over her the way he had? Every spot his body touched hers was suddenly achingly sensitive.

Her eyes were the softest, deepest brown, as fine as the powdered sand here at the lake bottom. As enticing as the watery depths. Those eyes held him spellbound, and her lips parted invitingly.

No, she wasn't indifferent. She was as curious as the little fish that still circled their boat.

Aleksy's body tightened in response. He could kiss her. He could close the gap and taste her, right here, right now.

They lurched apart, Aleksy smacking his elbow on the handlebars, and the captain banging her head into the glass.

"Baal!" she cursed, then composed herself and reached for the control panel. "We should collect a few samples and then return to the ship."

Aleksy could have kicked himself. No more lustful thoughts. Not now, not ever.

"That sounds very sensible."

Sensible. He could do that. He would be sensible for the remainder of their voyage. Hopefully.

Chapter 6

Captain's Log, 24 June, 1892
Lake Huron exploration, day 5. Tests successful. Areas marked for further exploration. Return to Detroit to proceed tomorrow as scheduled.

Nemo scooped up another bite of her dinner. Who would have thought green beans and boiled eggs could make such a delicious meal? A bit of garlic and onion, and a healthy dose of salt and pepper, and the bland foods became quite tasty. Best of all, she hadn't had to lift a finger.

"You're good at this vegetarian cooking business," she observed, waving the bean speared on her fork.

Aleksy shrugged. "I have to cook most of my own food. Everyone in my neighborhood thinks I'm strange to not eat meat. At home I eat a lot of bread and cheese."

And here as well. Every morning he'd eaten bread and cheese for breakfast. It was a good thing they were headed home tomorrow, because the cheese was nearly gone.

An unexpected pang twinged in Nemo's gut. She'd grown accustomed to his company this week. They worked well together, and she loved all the research he'd done into the microscopic life of the lake. Continuing on without him would be… strange.

But necessary. It wasn't as if he were her employee or

partner. He had a life elsewhere to return to. Bad enough she'd made him stay the week.

And she couldn't forget the other issues caused by his proximity. Every night since, she'd relived that near kiss in the Minersible. Sometimes scolding herself, sometimes imagining what might have been. It simply wouldn't do to let scientific excitement turn into excitement of a different kind. Her next mission would be a solo one. He would take his axolotl and leave.

"How is Nadia?" she asked.

Aleksy blinked at the change of subject. "Doing well. Her missing hand is regrowing nicely."

"Good. You're welcome to take one of the smaller specimen tanks with you to transport her when you leave the ship."

His brow wrinkled, only for a second, as if he'd momentarily forgotten he would be leaving. "Thank you."

"I have a plan for my return to the city, but we should also make a plan for your departure," Nemo said. It was the poised, sensible captain thing to do. Much better than questioning her growing sense of disappointment at the thought of striking out alone. "I anticipate an arrival in the city between three and four o'clock. Once we have docked, I will meet with my patron to deliver my reports and sign the final contracts for funding a full expedition. As smoothly as everything went, I don't expect it to take long."

Aleksy pushed food around on his plate without picking it up. "And we know they've been watching, so there will be no doubt you succeeded."

"Yes." When they'd returned to shallow waters this evening, they'd found that same boat with the mauve trim trailing after them. It couldn't possibly have followed them once they'd disappeared into deeper water, which meant it must have been waiting for them, all this time. Nemo twisted her earring with her free hand, a nervous habit she'd had since childhood. As usual, it didn't help. Apparently, she wasn't to be trusted.

Fine. Let them spy. They couldn't deny that she'd done as she'd promised. She'd earned her funding.

"Once my meeting is concluded, I will return here to the *Narwhal*," she continued. Poised. Sensible. Unperturbed by mistrustful men. "Then I will take you wherever you wish, either upriver or downriver. We can consult the map if it will help you choose a location. Perhaps a small city with a train station."

He nodded around a mouthful of food.

"Or, if you prefer, you can simply disembark in Detroit. If you wait until night falls, the docks will be empty. I don't think you'll be in any danger. Even if the police did discover what happened to you, I can't imagine they would be lying in wait. Not for a tiny crime that happened a week ago. My father wouldn't waste anyone's time for something so ridiculous."

Aleksy set down his fork. "I'm not afraid of the police. It's my employer who may be a problem."

Nemo lowered her fork as well. "Your employer is the man who hurt the axolotl?" She could understand Aleksy's concern. If a man could be cruel to an animal, what was to stop him showing that same cruelty to a fellow human?

Aleksy nodded. "Yes. I am—was—a janitor for the offices of the *Detroit Mirror* newspaper."

Nemo flinched. Her patron, Mr. Talon Stromberg, owned that paper. Surely he would know Aleksy's boss.

"I hear all the gossip," Aleksy continued. "I am no one. Part of the background. And because of my accent, they think I don't understand English."

Nemo huffed. Foolish to disregard a man for such reasons. And his English was stellar.

"I heard talk of strange animals," he went on. "Whispers of smuggling. I thought it silly until the day I saw fur on the chair in my employer's office. I began to pay more attention as I cleaned. I found hair, flakes of snake skin, scratch marks on the furniture. One day I heard the squawk of a bird through the closed door. I…" He heaved a sigh. "I began to snoop, to see if the rumors were true. I opened his books, read his papers."

Nemo slid forward in her seat. "And?"

"Most was nothing. Letters about the business. But one day I found an unsigned letter in a strange hand, speaking of delivering 'specimens.' It used the word 'experimentation.' I could not say this was for certain a terrible thing. You have seen me collect the tiny life from the lake and study it. I love science and I think observing animals and learning about them is important. But I had a bad feeling. This was so secret. I began to listen outside the office door when I could. The pieces of conversation I heard made me more concerned. Finally, one day, I saw that a tank had been placed in the room."

"The axolotl?"

He rubbed his temple. "Yes. She was not harmed when I first caught a glimpse of her. I ignored my duties to eavesdrop and heard part of a telephone conversation. Something about Natural Selection and the axolotl being a survivor. When I went in the next day, her limb had been amputated."

"So you think he's doing unethical experiments on these animals?" Nemo drummed her finger on the table. "Harming them to see how well they recover?"

"Yes. And perhaps making them fight one another. I went in the next day determined to do something. It was

Sunday morning, early, when no one is in the building but me. I unlocked the office, took Nadia, and hurried out. But apparently my employer had men watching and they chased me. I ran to the dock, fell into your boat." He shrugged. "I don't know if those men will still be looking for me, but they must suspect that I know about the animal smuggling."

"Damn." Nemo flopped against the back of the bench seat. Should she bring this up with her patron at the meeting? Tell him someone in his organization was involved in shady dealings? Would he even believe her? Her stomach knotted. Worse, what if Mr. Stromberg himself was the smuggler?

"Yes."

She collected herself. "Well, if you fear someone involved in this scheme might still be looking for you, I think the best plan is to wait for nightfall. The docks will be dark, and you can easily slip out unseen. What if I bring you a bicycle? Then you can ride home. It shouldn't be too hard to stick to streets without the bright arc lights. Will you be safe at home?"

He picked up his fork again, and resumed pushing the food around the plate without eating it. "I don't know. I hope so. I haven't anywhere else to go."

Nemo pursed her lips. "Here's what we'll do. You wait in the sub until dark. I'll bring a bicycle for you to ride home. I'd offer a ride in a steam car, but they're not as stealthy. Once you're home, if you're ever worried you're in danger, I can put you in touch with the police. No one should be allowed to harm you, even if you did steal something. I'll leave you my number. Do you have a telephone?"

Aleksy shook his head. "But there is one at the general store and one at the post office."

Not ideal, but it would do in an emergency. Her own household had three telephone lines. One for her, one for her parents, and one strictly for police business. It was good to remember that not everyone had the luxuries she did.

"Good," she said. "I think this will do. Chances are they're no longer searching for you. It's one small animal, and it sounds as though this man had many."

Aleksy's chest rose and fell in another heavy sigh. "I'm worried for the other animals."

"I'm sorry. Perhaps if you write down the things you saw and overheard you can file a report." Maybe she *should* report it to Stromberg. He would have enough political and social standing to get something done.

Unless he's the perpetrator.

He couldn't be. She would will him not to be. The entirety of her life savings had gone to the construction of this submarine. She needed his funding to pursue her research.

"I will think about writing a report on the matter," Aleksy replied. "Thank you. For both seeing to my welfare and allowing me to assist in your research. I very much enjoyed my unexpected voyage."

Heat began to rise in Nisha's cheeks, and she fought to keep herself collected. Again, the memory of the intimacy in the Minersible played in her mind. His ardent gaze. The press of his body.

"I enjoyed it as well," she said in the calmest voice she could muster. "It was good to have company."

He was leaving tomorrow. Captain Nemo could keep her cool that much longer.

Chapter 7

Captain's Log, 25 June, 1892
Arrival in Detroit. Test voyage successful.

Nemo stood atop her submarine, breathing in the fresh summer air. Semi-fresh, at least. Here at the docks there was always a lingering smell of river and commerce. A bit wet. A bit oily. Not enough to bother her, though. Not when she'd accomplished her task. She'd shattered all previous submarine records. Visited places no one ever had before.

All she had to do now was visit with her patron, finalize the paperwork, and then go home to celebrate with her family. Later, when night fell, she'd ride back to the docks and see Aleksy safely on his way. All perfectly straightforward.

She hopped up onto the dock and glanced back to check that the hatch was fully closed. She preferred the automatic closing mechanism for ensuring a proper seal, but when the ship was surfaced like this, she could do it manually.

Further downriver, a small steamship sat docked, bobbing slightly in the wake of other passing ships. Its distinctive mauve trim mocked her. All the way out and all the way back, they'd watched her. Ugh. There'd be no more of that, thank gods. She didn't need to prove herself any longer.

Nemo walked toward the business district until she

spied an unoccupied autocab chugging down the road. The driver gave her the raised eyebrow look that so many people gave any woman in trousers. Nemo ignored it and dropped a coin into the box.

"The *Detroit Mirror* building, please."

The driver nodded and the cab puffed off.

A short time later, she was striding beneath the wide front arch of the massive Neo-Romanesque *Detroit Mirror* building, captain's log and other papers in hand. She had visited Mr. Stromberg's office on the seventh floor once before, when they'd discussed the terms of her test voyage. Today, instead of taking the elevator, she climbed the stairs slowly, relishing the burn in her legs after too long with only the length of the submarine to walk.

The paneled oak door to the office stood ajar. A gleaming plaque affixed in the center announced, "Mr. Talon Stromberg, Owner." Nemo raised a hand to knock, but froze at the sound of conversation. Stepping away and waiting would be the polite thing to do, but her feet refused to move. She angled her ear toward the crack between the door and the jamb, and the words of the men inside the room became clearer.

Is this what Aleksy did? Is this where he stood, eavesdropping? Is Stromberg truly the smuggler?

"And the boy?" Stromberg's smooth voice inquired.

"Still on the submarine," an unknown man answered. "Hank is waiting, in case he tries to leave."

Nemo swallowed a gasp.

Stromberg made a rumbling almost-chuckle. "No. He will be stealthier than that. You underestimate his intelligence, I suspect. But even if you don't, it would be vastly foolish to underestimate *hers*. She will wait until dark, then sneak him off the ship or sail him to a nearby port."

The other man huffed. "You think he's smart but taking orders from a girl?"

"That 'girl' built my submarine. She's thwarted my men in the past. I prefer to exploit her skills, not fight them."

Nemo's heart thumped wildly. That scoundrel wanted her ship? The double-crossing scum!

"Yeah, sure," the minion agreed reluctantly. "So how do we catch the boy?"

Nemo didn't stick around to find out. She crept back to the stairs, then raced down, taking each corner so fast she arrived on the ground floor with her head spinning. Fighting to keep her equilibrium, she tore out into the street, waving at every autocab until one stopped for her.

She leapt aboard. "The docks. Hurry." She fumbled to get a coin into the collection box, then added a second one to emphasize the importance of speed.

The cab lurched into motion, rolling faster and faster until it was flying past the other vehicles on the street. Nemo offered up a prayer of thanks for steam engines and their massive amounts of torque.

When she reached the docks, she hopped out as recklessly as she'd hopped in, shouting a thanks to the driver. She ran toward the *Narwhal*, pulling up short a few hundred feet from where she was docked.

That man named Hank was here, somewhere, watching in case Aleksy disembarked. If he spied her acting suspiciously, word would get back to Stromberg.

Nemo took a calming breath, then adopted her usual stride. She walked to the *Narwhal*, boarded as she usually would, then ran to the controls.

Aleksy was seated in one of the library chairs, reading. He jumped when she rushed into the room.

"Captain? Is something wrong?"

Nemo flipped the switch to close and seal the hatch, raised the anchor, and started up the engine. Anyone watching would see the ship depart, but that couldn't be helped. She would need to rely on her head start. Fortunately, this time she didn't need to submerge. On the surface she'd be noticeably faster.

"Captain?" Aleksy asked again, rising from his seat.

"We need to leave immediately," she answered. "I'll explain later."

"But… I…" Words seemed to fail him. "Home?"

Nisha's chest tightened. She wouldn't be going home. Wouldn't see her family and her friends. She wasn't accustomed to long periods of time away, and certainly not to long periods of time without communication. With an enemy on her tail, would she even be able to stop long enough for a phone call or two? Probably not.

And poor Aleksy. His family had heard nothing from him but a single, short telegram. Assuming it had even reached its intended destination. Sending wireless telegrams from a submarine fell into the realm of experimental technology.

"You were right to be concerned," Nemo said as she steered the *Narwhal* upriver, heading back the way they'd come. "Talon Stromberg is after you."

"H-he is?" Aleksy walked to her side. "What happened? What did you see?"

Nemo kept her eyes on the river in front of her, pushing the *Narwhal* to a speed she would ordinarily deem imprudent in a high-traffic area.

"I didn't see. I heard. You would know, of course, that standing in the right place outside his office allows you to overhear conversations?"

"You went to his office? To check my story?"

"No. He's my patron." Nemo's jaw clenched. "I suppose he's not anymore. If he ever was. He wants my submarine. Probably to aid his smuggling. No wonder his tests were so concerned with speed and stealth." She kicked the base of the control panel, hard enough to startle Aleksy. "Goddammit! How could I have been so foolish?"

She knew the answer to that. She'd wanted it so much. True patronage would have made her dream possible, and she'd fallen into the fantasy.

"Your patron." Aleksy fell silent for a long moment. "I'm so sorry."

Nemo reached for the sense of serenity she always tried to wrap herself in; breathed in deeply, exhaled slowly. "I worried when you said you worked at the *Mirror*, but I didn't know the full truth until I heard Stromberg speaking to his lackey. Better to find out now than become further involved with him. And I'm sorry for you too. That boat following us? They've been watching for *you*. They had a man waiting on the docks."

"Kurwa," Aleksy muttered.

"If that means 'Fuck!' then I agree."

He laughed, despite the circumstances. "In the ways Americans use it, yes. In direct translation it is more like your word 'whore.'"

"Ah. We have a word like that in Bangla, too. Baal. Means 'pubic hair.' You may hear me say it on occasion. Don't tell my mother."

Aleksy's laugh turned into a snort. "Funny humans and our funny languages." He coughed and sobered. "What… er… what to do now?"

Nemo gave him an encouraging smile. "We flee. Regroup. Hopefully put enough space between us and them that we can consider our options. We can spend time below the surface to hide, but we need to dock somewhere for supplies. We need food and fuel. You need more clothing."

He rubbed his fuzzy jaw. "And shaving supplies."

"I think the beard looks nice."

He froze, his blue-gray eyes darkening. Despite the mess she'd made of his life, he still liked her, and right now he was looking at her as if she were as fascinating as one of his tiny specimens. Nemo snapped her attention back to piloting before she could do something foolish, like lick her lips or lean toward him.

Blast. She would have to contend with his proximity for longer than anticipated. It couldn't be helped. The only other option was to throw him to the wolves. Captain Nemo would never do such a thing to a crewmate.

And Nisha would never do such a thing to a friend.

Chapter 8

Captain's Log, 26 June, 1892
Lexington, Michigan. Noted for being a "charming resort town" with a "healthy lake breeze." Heading into port for restock of all needed supplies.

Aleksy lifted the periscope until it poked mere inches out of the water. He turned a slow circle, pausing to inspect each boat in sight. Nothing suspicious. No ships he'd seen before. He lowered the periscope and hurried to the bridge.

"Still no one following us, Captain," he reported. "Unless they have somehow tricked me. Absolutely no sign of the boat with the pink-purple stripe."

Nemo nodded. "I can't believe they would have given up their pursuit. We should remain vigilant when we disembark. But I think we're as safe as possible under the circumstances." She reached for the controls that would take the ship to the surface.

Aleksy remained at the helm, watching out the window as the *Narwhal* bubbled upward. He wondered what the other ships were thinking, seeing her rise up from the lake. Everyone in town would soon know of the strange vessel sailing into port.

"I'm going to dock there, at the far end of the harbor,"

Nemo said, pointing. "We'll be somewhat shielded from the view of anyone passing by."

"Good."

"As for the people here, I'm sure they'll have many questions. All we can do is be as friendly as possible."

"Yes. They won't want strangers coming into town and making trouble. We will be nice to them and buy their goods. Then they'll like us and dislike anyone who wishes to harm us."

"That's a highly optimistic outlook, Mr. Szekalski, but I like it."

Mr. Szekalski? Are we being formal again? Aleksy hoped he hadn't done anything to upset her. Well, anything more than ruin her potential funding and send her on the run from an enemy.

Perhaps the formality was warranted.

He said not a word while the submarine sailed into port and docked. It would be silly to mutter something as useless as, "I apologize for destroying your dream," or, "I didn't mean to put you in mortal peril." He longed to atone for all the trouble he'd caused, but at present he didn't even know if such a thing were possible.

"Here we are," Nemo announced, when the anchor was down. "Let's go into town. My stomach is rumbling. We'll have something to eat, buy everything we need, and then see about hiding for a few days while we figure out what to do."

"I have no money," Aleksy admitted. He was back in his own clothes today, but his pockets held not a single penny. He didn't have much money to begin with, and tended not to carry it unless deliberately going out to shop. In his close-knit neighborhood, many transactions were trades of goods or services instead of coin, in any case.

"I can cover expenses," Nemo replied. "My test voyage funds included enough for two full restocks of supplies."

"Ah, yes. But my personal things—"

"Are necessary crew supplies." Her tone wasn't angry, but it brooked no argument. She was the captain and she would pay.

Aleksy lapsed back into silence. What choice did he have? He couldn't continue wearing the same filthy clothing day after day. His week's worth of beard itched—although that particular annoyance was tempered by her statement that it looked good on him. New clothes and grooming supplies weren't optional, especially in the close quarters of the submarine. He would have to let her pay.

Possibly impossible to-do list: 1) apologize, 2) repay her.

Taking his silence for acceptance, the captain opened the hatch and disembarked. Aleksy climbed out after her, squinting in the sunlight and shielding his eyes. After a week indoors, he'd almost forgotten how bright a clear day could be. For a moment, he stood rooted in place atop the submarine, refamiliarizing himself with the warmth of the sun and the cool breeze off the water.

"Interesting ship you got there, lad," a voice called out.

Aleksy turned. A middle-aged man in the typical knit turtleneck and rubber boots of a sailor stood on the dock nearby, arms crossed over his chest.

"It's not my ship," Aleksy replied. "The lady is the captain."

The man's brow furrowed. "What's that?" He looked at Nemo. "Did he say *you* are the captain?"

"Indeed." Nemo bent over to close the hatch and snap a padlock into place. She tucked a key into the pocket of her vest before straightening up.

The sailor sniffed. "Huh. Gals in suits captaining weird ships? World's going downhill, I tell you."

Nemo ignored the slight. She stepped up onto the dock and motioned for Aleksy to join her. Eyes followed them as they walked toward town. Here and there, groups of men whispered. Some even nudged each other and pointed.

Nemo twisted the earring in her left ear as she let out a sigh of frustration. Another rare burst of emotion from the stoic captain. Aleksy repressed a sigh of his own. Why did it have to be the unpleasant feelings that grew so strong they broke through her barriers? He wanted to see more of her joy. Her excitement. The way she'd been before he foolishly almost kissed her.

He feared the days of glimpsing that side of her might be gone for good. Damn Stromberg and his crimes and treachery.

"This is why I prefer a big city," Nemo muttered. "Here I might literally be the only woman in trousers. In Detroit I'm merely 'one of *those* women.' Which isn't ideal, but it's better than being pointed at."

"I will pummel any man who insults you," Aleksy offered. He might have no money, but he was, as she'd pointed out, strong enough for manual labor. He could defend her honor.

"That's kind of you, but I thought we were trying to be friendly. We don't want to draw even more attention to ourselves. I suggest we remain calm unless someone behaves more hostile than curious."

"I will *absolutely* defend you from anyone hostile," Aleksy vowed. He owed her, and likely he would never be able to repay her. The least he could do was offer physical protection.

"If we can get what we need and be on our way before

Stromberg's men find us, your gallantry shouldn't be necessary." She strode toward a man who was neither whispering nor pointing. "Excuse me, where might we find a bite to eat in town?"

"You two from the city?" the man asked. "You'll want the Cadillac House hotel. Follow Huron Avenue straight up the hill."

"Thank you."

Aleksy and Nemo walked up the wide, packed-dirt street until they reached a large, well-maintained building where Huron met Main Street. Brightly painted letters mounted on the facade declared, "The Cadillac." They entered and crossed the lobby to the dining room. Ladies and gentlemen in their holiday finery filled the room, taking their mid-day meal at elegantly draped tables. Waitstaff in smart uniforms carried trays of steaming dishes. The scents of cooked meats and vegetables mingled in the air.

"This looks too fancy," Aleksy blurted. He couldn't let her pay for this. Not when he could barely stand letting her pay at all.

"It's not as stuffy as that," a voice spoke from over Aleksy's shoulder. "They'll even serve an old scallywag like me."

Aleksy turned to the man who had spoken. He had a face lined from years in the sun and a touch of gray in his brown hair, but his smile was boyish and his eyes bright. He wore the same style of turtleneck and boots as the sailors on the docks. A blue wool cap sat crookedly atop his unfashionably-long hair.

"They do allow me in, believe it or not," the man continued. "But that may be because I supply them with their venison. They cook it to perfection. You should try it."

"Venison," Aleksy repeated the unfamiliar word.

"Deer meat," Nemo murmured.

Aleksy blanched. "Er, no, thank you."

One of the uniformed women glided up to them. "Good afternoon, Mr. Merriman," she said to the sailor. "I have an open table for you and your friends, if you'd like to follow me."

"Uh…" Aleksy began. His gaze caught Nemo's, and she gave him a tiny shrug.

"Thank you, Verna," Merriman replied. "We'd be delighted."

The waitress led them to a table set for four. Aleksy took a seat between Nemo and the sailor. Strange as it was to sit down to lunch with a random stranger, there was a certain logic to it. Clearly Mr. Merriman was known in town. As a sailor, he would understand their supply needs. He would be able to point them to places where they could restock.

"Venison stew for you, Mr. Merriman?" Verna asked.

"Of course!" the sailor replied. "And a pint of your excellent ale."

Verna looked to Nemo and Aleksy. "Do you folks need to see a menu?"

"Do you have anything without meat?" Aleksy asked. No sense bothering with a menu if there weren't any vegetarian options.

The waitress frowned briefly. "The cook has a big pot of vegetable noodle soup simmering," she offered. "And there's salad."

Good enough. "One of each, please."

"I'll have the same," Nemo added. "And ale for each of us as well."

Aleksy sent her an appreciative smile.

"So…" Merriman drawled. "You two sailed in here on

the most curious vessel." A covetous gleam flashed in his eyes. "I'd love to hear all about it."

Aleksy tried not to squirm. Was this man trustworthy? Perhaps he thought Nemo was an easy target due to her sex. Maybe he was a pirate who meant to seize their ship. Aleksy shook off the thought. No, that was ridiculous. What sort of pirate would be having a casual lunch in a tiny lakeside town? Still, he was glad to be sitting in between the captain and the stranger. He wouldn't forget his promise to defend her.

Nemo addressed Merriman with her usual placid manner. "The *Narwhal* is a submarine. On an experimental research voyage. If she performs well, perhaps I will license my design to a shipbuilding company, so that additional submarines can explore our beautiful lakes."

"Wonderful!" Merriman exclaimed. "As a fellow sailor, I am intrigued and delighted with all new sailing technologies. I would love to someday see how she operates." This time, a touch of his hunger crept into his voice. Either this man wanted the *Narwhal,* or he wanted a ship like her.

Kurwa. Maybe he is *a pirate.*

"We haven't time to give tours, I'm afraid." Nemo's smile was amiable, but her tone was one of command. "We're here to gather supplies and then we must be off."

"Ah." Merriman lounged against the back of his chair. "Perhaps another time, then. You'll be needing fuel, I assume? Coal? Is she steam powered?"

"She is. We need fuel, food, and a place to purchase clothing and other personal items. Do you have any recommendations?"

Merriman gave them a list of shops, even going so far as to advise, "Don't let old Gandy cheat you. He likes to give higher prices to out-of-towners. Tell him Tom Merriman sent you and he'll give you the local price."

After that, the food arrived, and the conversation settled into generic sea-faring talk of weather, currents, traffic, and so forth. Aleksy sipped at his soup and didn't contribute much. He couldn't shake the feeling that Merriman wasn't entirely trustworthy. Was it wrong to be contemplating possible ways to defend oneself with a spoon?

Nemo remained her imperturbable self. Now and then, however, she did reach up to fiddle with the diamond in her ear. A nervous habit? Aleksy would have plenty of time to observe and find out. Only God knew how long they would be on the submarine together now.

Dammit. He needed to send another message to his mother, to say that he wouldn't be returning home after all. He hoped she wasn't stomping around cursing his name. Or worse, kneeling in church, clutching her rosary and praying for him to recover his senses and go home like a good boy.

"There's a telegraph office in town, yes?" he asked the pirate—sailor.

"At the train station," Merriman answered.

"Thank you."

"My pleasure." His smirk made Aleksy twitch. What if he was lying to them? What if he meant to seize their ship while they wandered around town, sent to all the wrong places?

His fears proved unfounded. The directions Merriman had supplied were accurate, and the shops he recommended were full of all the things they needed. Two hours later, they stood on the dock beside the *Narwhal*, supervising a pair of local youths as they assisted with the two full cartloads of goods Nemo had purchased. Aleksy clutched the sturdy suitcase filled with new clothing. She'd spent well over one hundred dollars on him, and the burden of repaying such a sum now sat like a lead weight in his belly. He had to do something to make it up to her. Anything less was unthinkable.

He passed the suitcase down the hatch to Nemo and then reached to take another box of supplies from one of the boys.

Maybe it's me, he considered. *Maybe I can't accept help. That's why I feel a gnawing guilt every time she does something for me. That's why I ascribed criminal motivations to a man who was being entirely friendly and helpful.*

When everything was loaded, Nemo climbed back out to pay the boys and send the carts on their way. She made a quick check of the exterior of the ship, then waved Aleksy toward the hatch.

"Time to go."

"Good luck to you!" Merriman's voice called out. Aleksy turned to spot him a few docks over, standing beside a plain, but seaworthy steamboat.

"Thank you, Captain," Nemo called back. "If you ever need a favor in return, you need only ask."

Even from this distance, Aleksy could make out the sailor's smug expression. "Oh, I will, darling," Merriman replied. "I will."

"Is it bad that I don't trust him?" Aleksy whispered.

Nemo's brows arched. "Bad? I think it would be worse if you *did* trust him. Haven't you heard of Tom Merriman before?"

"No." Aleksy drew the word out.

"Oh. I just assumed from your constantly clenched fists…" She gave Merriman a final wave, then began the climb down into the submarine. "He's the only man to have ever been charged with piracy on the Great Lakes," she explained, then dropped out of sight.

Chapter 9

Captain's Log, 26 June, 1892
Supplies restocked. May owe a favor to a pirate.

Nemo checked the depth gauge. Sixty fathoms. Not as deep as she would have liked, but it would do for tonight. It was her own fault they hadn't had time to sail into the deep northern portion of the lake. She could have been more efficient about supplies. Bought a few less things. Eaten on the go instead of sitting down in a restaurant to chat with a pirate.

She hadn't quite decided whether lunch with Merriman had been a brilliant idea or a terrible one. He'd been a pleasant companion, despite his less-than-savory occupation. He definitely coveted her ship, but he'd spoken with her as an equal, without seeming to care that she was a brown-skinned woman. The advice he'd given had been accurate and helpful. That was worth a future favor, right?

Nemo had wanted to be an explorer for as long as she could remember. She had a massive collection of atlases and books from and about all parts of the world. She'd once been the girl who walked around Detroit marking all the most interesting spots on her hand-drawn map. Even so, a life of exploration was turning out to be more tumultuous than she'd anticipated.

Fortunately, she was nothing if not tenacious. She was her Dadi's granddaughter, through and through.

She let the anchor down and shut off all non-essential systems for the night. Her stomach rumbled. She'd been too busy pushing for deeper water to stop for dinner. Hopefully Aleksy would have something waiting for her. Probably he would. She couldn't claim to know him well yet, but their week together had shown him to be a conscientious man. Not the sort to let a woman go hungry.

"I saved you some food," he announced when she stepped into the next room, proving her correct.

She slid onto the bench and pulled the bowl toward her. He'd mixed chickpeas with diced onions and tomatoes, and topped it all with a tangy vinegar-based dressing. Tasty. Perhaps she could get him to try making some of her mother's recipes. He might do a better job of it than Nemo did.

"Thank you," she said. "This is excellent. I've dropped anchor and shut her down for the night. I thought we might discuss plans before we go to bed."

She quickly looked down at her food to avoid any eye contact that might make him interpret her words as innuendo. They hadn't been, but she needed to be more careful with her word choice. No mentions of beds. No mentions of personal things. Nothing that could be interpreted as flirtatious.

"What are you thinking?" Aleksy asked.

Nemo froze. Several seconds passed before she realized he was asking about her plans for dealing with their villain. Not wondering about her seductive fantasies. Dammit, what was wrong with her?

"Nothing. I have no good ideas," she admitted. She lifted her gaze to meet his. Enough with the ridiculous fretting. He'd been a true gentleman the entire time she'd known him. If he hadn't kissed her when they'd been nearly in each other's laps, he probably never would.

"All I can think to do is hide." Aleksy rubbed his jaw. He'd shaved off the stubbly beard, but he was equally handsome with and without it.

Dammit, Nisha.

"Hiding is a good start," she said. "Since we're the only ship that can dive to the bottom of the lake, Stromberg can't follow us. We could even sail around into Lake Michigan and hide there. Lake Superior is extremely deep, but I'm not sure we want to go there yet. We'd have to pass through the locks, and everyone would talk about the strange boat that went by. But even with only two lakes, I believe we can sneak around until they no longer know our whereabouts."

Aleksy nodded. "And then?"

"That's the part where I have no idea. If we wait long enough will he give up on chasing us?"

Aleksy's only reply was a doubtful expression.

"I could drop you off somewhere far from home. Chicago, or somewhere in Wisconsin. You could make your way home by train." She idly fingered an earring. "But would you be safe to return or would he be waiting? And what about my ship? I suspect he wants it for his smuggling. Ugh. I see no good options."

Aleksy slumped in his seat. "I'm so sorry. I wish I hadn't made all this trouble."

Nemo leaned across the table. No. She was not going to let him blame himself for this. "There was always trouble. All you did was bring it to my attention. Stromberg is a villain. What we need is a way to thwart him."

How did one thwart a powerful media mogul? His damned newspaper was always printing lurid stories. Ironically, stories about smuggling and other crimes were among the most popular. Too bad they couldn't get the paper to run a story about the owner's misdeeds. They could write to a rival paper, but Stromberg would merely print his own story refuting it. And perhaps sue for libel.

"Do you know of any evidence against Stromberg we could report to the police?" Nemo asked. "We could send it to my father. Stromberg must believe you know something important to be chasing after you. He wouldn't put forth all that effort just to get the axolotl back."

"I don't know." Aleksy stared off into the distance, thinking. "I saw so many papers. Contracts. Lists of payments. They may be part of his real business. Only the letter about the experiments surprised me."

"And one vaguely worded letter that may not even exist any longer isn't enough to send the police after him. Damn."

"I'm sorry. I will try to think about it and write down anything I remember."

"Good. I may send a telegram to my friends back home and ask them to research Stromberg. My friends Victor and Mary have a lawyer who's good at finding things. And Callie knows scandalous secrets about many of the city's elite. In the meantime, we can resume our studies. We may as well make the most of our time hiding in the lakes."

And keeping busy will help banish other, less appropriate thoughts from my brain.

"I would like that. I enjoyed researching last week."

"So did I."

Nisha turned her attention to her dinner. Aleksy cleaned up and stowed the cooking equipment and his own dishes before making his goodnights and heading to the bunk room. At least he had proper clothes and supplies now. The crew bunks were narrow and the room spartan. She'd thought to use the extra beds for friends or family joining her for a short jaunt. Or for research crew who accepted the simple accommodations willingly. Aleksy had literally fallen into this.

Nemo cleaned her own dinner things, then walked down the hall, slipping past the curtain into her captain's quarters. The space wasn't luxurious, but it contained a desk, a sink and a mirror for washing and dressing, and a bed that was easily twice as wide as the crew bunks. Plus the mattress was thicker and the quilt softer. It seemed suddenly painfully unfair that she could sprawl out here, where there was room for two…

She flung herself on the bed with a groan. This had to stop. Wasn't there a doctor in Battle Creek who claimed rich and spicy foods inflamed lustful appetites? Maybe that was the solution. She'd try eating plain bread and nothing else.

Nisha changed into her nightgown and crawled into bed. Closing her eyes, she concentrated on her breathing. In, out. In, out. She pushed away the world outside and connected with her body, relaxing muscles tight from a day of stress. Eventually, she sank into a deep slumber.

* * *

Clang!

Aleksy bolted upright so fast he hit his head on the bunk above him.

Clang!

The sound vibrated straight through the hull of the submarine and left his ears ringing. Whatever had caused the noise had struck the ship directly above him.

Clang!

He leapt from the bed and darted into the hall. "Capt—"

The curtain across the way slid aside, and he sprang back in surprise. In the dim corridor, she looked like a ghost, all swathed in white.

"Captain, I... I think something's hit us."

The clanging sounded again, no longer directly overhead, but still nearby. Was some foolish ship dragging an anchor? Had they drifted from their own resting place into some rocks? Were they under attack?

Another clang shook the ship, the sound slightly further away than before.

"What the hell is happening?" Nemo cursed, her voice thick and groggy. She lifted a hand to rub her eyes.

"I think someone is hitting us." Aleksy walked down the hall, in the same direction the noises seemed to be moving. When the next crash happened above him, he knew he'd guessed correctly. "They're banging into us. Over and over. Moving along the ship."

Nemo cursed again, sounding fully awake now. "They're feeling us out," she guessed. "Using an anchor or other dangling implement to map our size and location."

"Why? To prove they've found us and not... a rock?" He winced as another collision echoed down the corridor.

Nemo whirled toward the control room. "Or to prepare for dropping something else on us."

His entire body went rigid with terror. "Something... explosive?" he choked out.

The captain raced toward the front of the ship, talking as she went. "Or it's a hook and they're trying to find a place to snag us!"

Aleksy's muscles woke slowly. He shuddered, then hurried after her. "Do you think they could pull us out of the water?"

"With a large and powerful steamship, maybe. But if anything catches on our propeller, it could destroy the ship. Help me get her ready to flee."

"What do you need me to do?"

Nemo jerked a hand at the controls. "Pull up the anchor. I'll start her up."

Aleksy reached for the lever, thankful for the times he'd watched her do this very thing. Beside him, Nemo pushed buttons and flipped switches. The distant whir of the propeller joined the cacophony of their enemy's attack.

"Watch the echo sensor. I'm going to drive us as fast as she can go." She shoved the throttle forward and grabbed the wheel.

Aleksy flattened his hands on either side of the light display, trying to make sense of it. Most of the circle was dark, but an oval of lights in the center gave off a dim glow.

"Faint light in the center," he reported.

"The ground beneath us. Stop me if it glows too bright. Warn me of anything in the surrounding areas."

Aleksy nodded. He wasn't sure if the captain noticed. She'd turned on none of the main lights, inside or out, leaving them to work only by the small nightlights in the floor and ceiling. The glow from various dials and controls illuminated her hands and cast odd shadows across her face. He turned his gaze back to the display and let her work.

The clanking ceased as the *Narwhal* sped off into the darkness. For how long, he couldn't guess. He could only do his job.

They quickly fell into a pattern. Report and respond.

"All lights are off."

"Descending."

"Bright light on the left."

"Port. Adjusting course."

"Left—port—lights are gone. Dim lights below."

"Holding steady."

The only clock to mark the time was the beating of Aleksy's heart. On and on they went into inky blackness, speeding northward and downward until his limbs began to cramp up from holding in the same position. Out of habit he glanced down at his wrist, but of course he didn't have his watch. It was too fragile and precious to wear while sleeping.

Nemo eased the throttle back, bringing the ship to a halt. She flipped a few more switches, and silence descended.

"Hopefully we've lost them," she whispered.

There was no need to whisper. No one on the surface could ever hear them, even if they shouted. Somehow, though, speaking in anything but hushed tones seemed the height of folly. Even his breathing sounded unnecessarily loud in the stillness.

The lights on the display before him were dark, the wide bank of windows a vast plain of nothing. He closed his eyes and listened, straining to pick up any sound that might suggest the enemy could still find them, still reach them.

Nothing. Only emptiness. Only quiet.

His other senses sharpened. The hint of something floral touched his nose. Cold seeped up from the metal floor, chilling his bare feet. Warmth radiated from the body beside him.

Alesky's eyes flew open. Had he been standing this close to Nemo the entire time?

Vaguely, he remembered their arms bumping or brushing as they'd worked side-by-side. Now, though, they were at rest, but still nearly touching. The few glowing dials provided enough light to make out her tumbling hair and the simple nightgown she wore.

Jezu Chryste.

It didn't matter that the gown was buttoned to her neck and had long sleeves. It was one, single layer of fabric, clinging to her body. Her feet were also bare, her toes peeking out from beneath the almost-floor-length hem.

Aleksy's pulse had hardly begun to slow, and now it was off to the races once again.

"Nisha," he breathed, using her given name for the first time. She'd only said it the once, but he hadn't forgotten. It meant "night," according to one of the books he'd skimmed during his week here. Perfect for her. Beautiful. Mysterious. Full of possibility.

He let his head drop toward hers, even knowing it was a bad idea. He shouldn't kiss her. It was wrong. Beyond improper.

He had to stop. He had to pull away before the frenzy of their escape caused him to do something he couldn't take back.

Before he could force his body to respond, she rose up on her toes and pressed her lips to his.

Chapter 10

Captain's Log, 27 June, 1892
In deeper waters. Nothing further to report.

The kiss was as whisper-quiet as the motionless submarine. Nisha's lips moved across his in a soft, careful exploration. Aleksy responded in kind, his hands settling on her back as he eased his body flush against hers.

Each gentle touch sent spikes of pleasure zinging across her skin. He was warm, solid, comforting. Heat and light in the midst of perpetual cold and dark. A precious relief from the night's troubles.

Although he was an altogether different sort of trouble.

Nemo laced her fingers together behind his neck, unable to compel herself to break the embrace. Her tongue glided across his lower lip in slow, easy strokes. Tasting. Testing. He opened for her, his mouth mimicking her languid movements.

She couldn't hold back a sigh. How could a gentle, soothing kiss be so volatile? Desire boiled inside her. The tiny, unhurried sweeps of his tongue coaxed moans from low in her throat. Her body cried for more, even as she relaxed into the sweet mingling of lips and mouths.

Kissing Aleksy Szekalski was a study in physical science. He was all potential energy, stored up and waiting.

Exactly the way he was in his daily life. Nemo had quickly grown accustomed to his quiet presence, whether he was reading, studying, or merely watching her work. But it was always punctuated with bursts of excitement. She never knew when he might come racing onto the bridge, babbling about feathery appendages on microscopic creatures, passion on full display.

That was this kiss. Not mild, not boring, but a tightly wound ball of lust, teetering on the edge of a steep embankment.

Nisha knew the instant gravity won. Aleksy's fingers tightened on her nightgown and his head tipped to change the angle of the kiss. Their bodies crushed together. Her nipples tightened as her breasts rubbed against his chest. She squirmed a little, eager for more friction.

Aleksy took control of the kiss, thrusting his tongue further between her lips, delving into her mouth as if he could never have enough of her. Nisha slid her hands up to tangle in his hair. The cool captain was gone. She was on fire and she would happily let herself burn down to ashes.

She squirmed again, with more deliberation this time, rocking their hips together and enjoying the burgeoning bulge in his trousers.

He drew back with a sharp hiss of breath. "I shouldn't…" He appeared momentarily at a loss for words. "Shouldn't touch you."

Nisha brushed her hair back behind her ears. "I see nothing wrong with mutually agreeable ravishment."

The moment the words were out of her mouth, her brain began to formulate a list of all the reasons not to continue. Just because it wasn't wrong didn't mean it was a good idea.

You didn't think this through beforehand. You have no contraception. You don't want to risk hurting his feelings or yours. You have other, more important concerns. You're stuck here together for an unknown duration.

"It's very late," Aleksy said. "We are tired and we were scared. Maybe we can talk in the morning?"

Nisha nodded. "Yes," she added, to make sure he understood her, even in the faint light. "We should return to bed. It's important we get enough rest."

Another reason to add to her list. Choosing sex over sleep was illogical when you were on the run from an enemy.

Aleksy still stood close enough that she could see his chest rise and fall as he took a deep breath. "Goodnight, Captain," he said. He inclined his head, then turned and walked off.

Nemo waited a moment before following. A shiver trembled through her. Already she missed his warmth. She'd been gone from her bed long enough for the sheets to cool. She hurried to her cabin and piled blankets atop herself.

How long would she have to wait until the sensible decision began to feel like the correct one? An hour? All night?

She slept fitfully, eventually rolling out of bed an hour earlier than her customary time. A longer-than-usual shower only somewhat soothed her, and she let herself pretend it was lingering anxiety from the attack. They would have to stay deep today, and pick an unpredictable path so no one watching from above could locate them when they inevitably returned to shallower waters.

Nemo hauled on a sturdy, olive green boiler suit and laced up her favorite boots. Back to work. She would mark down the kiss as a temporary aberration. They would resume their amiable, but uncomplicated alliance.

Aleksy sat at the dining table, munching on his usual bread and cheese. He'd dressed in some of his new clothing:

a plain white shirt and dark gray trousers. No vest, no coat, no tie. He'd left the shirt open at the collar and rolled up the sleeves to his elbows.

Nemo's throat went dry.

He's chosen practical working garb, she scolded herself. *He is not trying to entice you with his muscular forearms.*

He took a quick gulp of water to wash down his food, then spoke. "Would you like me to apologize for last night?"

Nemo walked to the pantry to fetch the fried poori and the spicy chutneys she liked to dip it in. It was all better fresh, but still made a satisfactory breakfast when preserved for storage. Her supply was dwindling, but hopefully she could stretch it out until they could return to Detroit.

"I began the kiss," she declared. "I take full responsibility. No sense dwelling on it."

There. That sounded reasonable.

As she turned toward the table, she caught a flicker of disappointment on Aleksy's face before he shuttered it and returned to his breakfast.

A pang of regret stabbed her gut. She hadn't meant to hurt him. Her words had been too blasé. She considered offering up a more comprehensive explanation. The kiss had been spectacular. Even now, thinking of it made her body hum in anticipation. Under other circumstances, she would delight in repeating it. Here and now, though, they had more pressing concerns than giving free rein to their unsated libidos.

"We will stay deep today?" he asked, before she could voice any of her thoughts.

"Yes."

"Good. I think they can't find us here." He stared off into the distance as Nemo slid into her own seat. "Maybe your idea to drop me off in Wisconsin was good," he added, after a long pause. "If Stromberg is after us both, he will have to split his attention. It will be easier to avoid his men."

Nemo made herself nod. "And once you're on land you can telephone the police and your family, or anyone else who might be of assistance. They can all be prepared before you arrive. I think you're right."

She jabbed a piece of poori into the small jar of sauce. Dammit. He was absolutely right. Going separate ways wasn't safe, precisely, but it was a better option than anything else they had so far. They couldn't stay underwater forever.

Aleksy ate the last of his food, then rose to clean and put away his dishes. "Do you need my assistance today, Captain? If not, I will study more samples and compare them with what I found before. I would like to continue my research while I am here."

"Please do. I appreciate your work."

She finished her breakfast quickly, then went to the helm to plot her course. Today they would follow a winding path through the deepest area of the lake. That would give her time to prepare for a quick dash through the Straits of Mackinac, perhaps at night, to aid with stealth. Once in Lake Michigan, she could spend more time hiding in the depths before choosing the best landing point to drop Aleksy off. In a matter of days, they would part, likely forever.

It *was* the best plan. Logical. Sensible. Exactly what a level-headed captain would choose.

Maybe she wasn't the self-possessed captain she'd thought she was. Because her heart screamed a different truth. She'd driven him away. One kiss, and she'd ruined everything.

Chapter 11

Captain's Log, 29 June, 1892
Excellent progress on Lake Huron cartography project. Still no signs of anyone following us.

Aleksy peered into the microscope. The tiny life form in the droplet swam in circles. Probably confused, poor thing. He consulted his notes, flipped back a few pages, then checked the microscope again. Another match. He studied the wriggling creature, noting the shape, size, movement.

He poured the droplet from the slide back into the insulated cup where he held his samples while studying them. The water would be dumped back into the lake when he was finished. He wasn't sure whether all his little zoo-plankton survived the journey in and out of the submarine, but he did his best not to harm them. He would not be like Stromberg.

Aleksy flipped through his notes again, comparing the copepod he'd observed to those from other samples. It definitely matched samples 15A, and 8E, and 7C. Similar to 14B, 15B, and 12D: a copepod from Order Calanoida. But not the same species.

His pulse sped up. Could this truly be something new? He'd seen four of them now: too many to assume the differences were a mutation, especially given the various locations of the samples. He grabbed the reference book on freshwater biology he'd taken from Nemo's library and turned to the relevant section. Skimming a finger down the page, he reviewed the list of copepods. Few species had accompanying pictures, but each entry contained a short description. He found the calanoids and read carefully. Not one description matched the species he'd found.

Aleksy hurried to the front of the book to check the publication date. The book was brand new, published this year. It was as up-to-date a reference as he was likely to find.

He sprang from his seat, snatching up his notebook and hugging it to his chest. A new species! He'd discovered a new species! This could get him accepted in the biological community. It could help Nemo find funding from a new patron.

He was halfway across the room before the rational part of his brain broke through the excitement. Barging into her control room shouting about tiny crustaceans would be entirely inappropriate. This was business, and he needed to remember that.

A now-familiar pang of loss struck him. Avoiding one another was impossible within the confines of the submarine, but a noticeable distance had grown between them these past two days. Their conversation was polite, but impersonal, focused on the information they needed to share for their work. He'd taken care to keep a larger physical distance between them. The last thing he wanted was for her to fear he might touch her again.

Keeping his stride slow and even, he walked into the control room. Nemo sat at the helm, but she wasn't actively steering. Several maps lay open atop the controls, along with a compass and a ruler. The captain had a pencil in hand, marking information on the map in front of her.

Aleksy waited for her to pause before speaking. "Good afternoon, Captain. I trust your project is going well?"

She swiveled her chair around to face him. "It is. With all the data I've collected, this new map of the lake will be the most detailed and accurate ever made. How are your studies?"

He opened his notebook to his most recent sketch. "I believe I've discovered a new species."

Nemo's dark brown eyes widened and she hopped out of her chair. "A new species? Truly?"

Aleksy thrust the book out at arm's length, not daring to move any closer.

Her excitement is for science. Not for you.

She accepted the book, her movements once again calm. Her eyes, however, remained large and luminous as she peered at his drawings.

"You can see the unknown species there," he said, "including my notes about physiology and behavior. If you turn back to the page about sample 8E, there is another drawing."

"And you couldn't find this particular creature in the reference books?"

"No. Even the most comprehensive of the books doesn't list it."

Her smile grew as she read over his notes, and her fingers flipped the pages with swift, eager movements. No captain's facade could conceal her excitement entirely.

"It looks like a grain of rice with hairy antennae," she remarked. Her lips made a tiny twitch.

Aleksy wanted to groan in a mix of desire and frustration. Why did he have to be so attuned to her? She didn't want him. Their kiss may have left him a smoldering wreck, but it clearly hadn't been the same for her. He would respect her wishes and keep their relationship strictly professional. Even if the close quarters left him in constant torment.

"Most copepods do, from above," he replied. "For this particular species, the antennae are genticulated—bent. I wrote down the length and location of the bends, and the size and number of caudal spines. If you turn the page there is a side view. It will look more like a shrimp, and you'll see my notes about the legs and other body features."

She glanced up at him, her perfect lips making another small upward twitch. "You're very thorough."

Damn that smile. She was going to kill him without meaning to.

"Thank you." The words came out terse and slightly gruff.

Fortunately, she either didn't notice his discomfort or she ignored it. "Is there anything I can do to help with this? Do you need more samples? Other data?"

"I'd like the coordinates of the places we stopped for samples, our depth, and the water temperature, if you have it."

"Of course! Here. Take a look at my map."

Aleksy stepped up to the control panel beside her, the closest he'd been since their kiss. He angled his body so he wouldn't crowd her, before leaning over the map.

"There are the locations where we paused for samples and measurements," Nemo said, pointing. "Here's your sample fifteen. We were at ninety-six fathoms, and the temperature was thirty-nine point eight degrees." She handed him his notebook, then offered her pencil. "Shall we go through all your samples?"

Aleksy quickly jotted the latitude and longitude, along with the other numbers. Nemo took him through their course, point-by-point, to make sure he didn't miss anything.

By the time he was done, he'd relaxed enough not to flinch away when her arm bumped his. Maybe this wasn't so bad. He could go back to being friends and forget the kiss ever happened.

"If you'd like I can add the pressure, terrain type, and other information next time we stop for a sample," Nemo offered. "I want you to have all the data you need. This discovery is going to be incredible. You'll get your name in all the biology books!" This time, she didn't try to keep her enthusiasm from her voice.

Aleksy felt heat rise in his cheeks. "I hope it will bring *you* attention. When people see what we can learn with your submarine, they will all want to fund your research. I will tell everyone how amazing you are."

She spun to face him, eyes shining. "You would use your discovery to help me?"

"Yes," he answered, with no hesitation. "I would never be here without you. We should share the honor."

"Thank you," she murmured.

Was it his imagination, or was she leaning toward him? He held perfectly still, barely daring to breathe. Her lips were parted and her eyes dark with desire. Not the look of a woman who'd hated his kiss.

She didn't touch him, but she didn't step away, either. When she at last straightened, putting a bit of space between them, the motion was relaxed and slow. Her smile remained friendly.

"I should let you get back to your research," she said. "You should nap this afternoon, if you're able. Tonight we'll sail through the Straits of Mackinac to Lake Michigan. I'm planning to go as fast as possible in the hopes of getting back into deep water undetected."

Once again, she was Captain Nemo, practical leader,

but this side of her was no longer as aloof as it had once been. Her tone was warmer, her smile more genuine. Aleksy would never have noticed the subtle shift if he hadn't spent days upon days alone with her.

She's not indifferent. She didn't hate our kiss.

He'd misread her earlier. Had she only kept her distance because he'd been doing the same? What did this mean for their relationship?

Aleksy couldn't deny that they had a connection and an attraction. Certainly, he liked her well enough to want to explore. Maybe whatever they had could evolve into something new. Something extraordinary. He would never push himself on her. But from now on there would be no holding back, either.

Only a few days remained before they would part ways. And he didn't want to leave wondering what-if.

Chapter 12

Captain's Log, 30 June, 1892
Have reached Straits of Mackinac. Continuing on overnight.

The *Narwhal* sped on, following the narrow channel in the middle of the strait, where the water was deepest. Nemo paused to wipe her hands on her trousers. Almost there. Another hour and they would be far enough into Lake Michigan to dive a little deeper and get some rest. Tonight's mission had gone well. She only needed to keep doing what she'd been doing.

"There's something ahead and slightly on the… left side, Captain," Aleksy reported. He'd given up any attempt at using the nautical terms. Nemo wasn't going to press him on it. Directions didn't seem to be his forte.

Nemo glanced at the echo-reader. The far edge of the circle registered something in front of them. She pulled back on the throttle to slow the ship, then flicked on her lantern to check her map. The red-tinted light allowed her to read the chart without ruining her dark vision.

"We're still on course. According to the map, there shouldn't be anything there."

She eased off on the throttle even more, then looked at Aleksy. The red light illuminated a brow crinkled in worry.

"That's not good," he replied.

"We'll approach slowly, in case it's an enemy trap. I'm going to take her up a few fathoms to put us at periscope depth."

He made a curt nod, then turned his attention back to the display in front of him.

Baal! This was what she got for letting herself think things were going well.

Maybe she'd been lulled into a false sense of security by the ease of her collaboration with Aleksy. The awkwardness that they'd suffered the last few days had disappeared after he'd shared his discovery. She'd even stopped berating herself for handling the aftermath of their kiss so poorly. Naturally, the world would choose this time to throw a wrench into her plans.

She pressed on, bringing the *Narwhal* slightly to starboard in case they needed to navigate around the obstacle ahead. At this slow speed, the *chug-chug* of the steam engine was little more than a whisper. No one would hear or see them coming. If this was an enemy trap, stealth was her only real weapon.

"Can you check the periscope?" she asked. "I can keep an eye on all the displays at this speed."

Aleksy hurried off without a word. A few minutes later, he jogged back into the room.

"There's a single ship. Nothing else, but there's no moon, so it's hard to see. Can we go closer? Or is that not safe?"

Nemo frowned down at her indicators. "A ship shouldn't register as directly in front of us unless it sank, or is dragging something underneath it. We'll move closer. Keep an eye out and let me know when you can see more."

"Aye." He gave her a crooked salute and dashed off.

The submarine crept onward. Nemo's fingers grazed the switch for the exterior lights. The echo sensor was the most sophisticated piece of machinery on the entire vessel. A decade of work had gone into perfecting it. Even so, the inability to rely on her own eyes to see what lay ahead made her twitch. She stared out the window anyway, as if she could make something appear out of the bluc-black nothing by force of will.

Her gaze dropped to the control panel, checking and rechecking their position and distance from the nearby anomaly. Why had she thought of the water as blue-black? Shouldn't it be nothing but black in the moonless night?

Her head snapped up. The water in front of her *was* bluish, and growing bluer by the second. Whatever was in front of her had powerful lights.

Pounding footsteps caused her to spin her chair around. Aleksy raced into the room.

"Update on the ship, Captain. It has two tall poles with sails, but also a smokestack and propeller. It's not moving."

"Sounds like a standard merchant steamship," Nemo replied. Or a pirate. Merchants didn't sit around at night shining strange lights underwater.

Aleksy walked up until he was standing directly beside her. "Is something… glowing outside?"

"It appears so, yes. Whoever that is up there, they›re doing something underwater. In the middle of the night."

"Suspicious." He met her gaze and held it. "Do we run away, or do we go close enough to look?"

They stood there for a long moment, as the ship glided nearer and the water grew lighter. They both knew the answer. This ship was built for exploration. It didn't leave mysteries unsolved.

Within seconds, the scene materialized in front of them. Nemo brought the submarine to a full stop and leaned toward the windows.

Bright beams of light shone down from the ship floating up on the surface. An enormous hatch in the hull of the ship hung open. A massive metal claw stretched down from the opening, its wide, multi-toothed talons clamped around what appeared to be the battered remains of an old train car.

"Merriman," Nemo breathed. A pirate then, not an enemy. Not ideal, but better than it could have been.

"The pirate from Lexington?"

"It has to be. He's known for raising whole sections of shipwrecks and plundering whatever he finds. No one ever knew how he did it, though."

Aleksy gestured at the window. "Now we know. With a special boat and a giant machine."

The claw trembled, but didn't release or lift its cargo. Was it stuck? She looked up at the ship. The propeller churned up the water, and the engine rumbled. The ship rocked side-to-side.

"They're stuck," she said. "Either that wreck they're trying to lift is more firmly embedded in the ground than they thought, or the claw is wedged into the rocks."

"Or both."

Nemo's hands were moving to the surfacing controls before her brain had even fully processed the decision. "I'm taking her up. We'll signal to Merriman and offer our assistance. The Minersible is small and nimble enough to go down there and look for the problem."

Aleksy's brows knit together. "You want to offer to help a pirate?"

"I owe him a favor after his assistance the other day. I'd rather repay it sooner than later."

"Very well." Aleksy blew out a breath. "Tell me what to do."

The moment the submarine hit the surface, Nemo flicked

the switch for the signal lamp. She tapped out a greeting in Morse Code.

Captain. Good to see your sub again, came the reply.

Do you need help? Nemo asked.

My salvage machine is trapped. Can your ship see the problem?

No. But I have a submersible. I can get closer and try to unstick you.

I would appreciate it.

Hold in place. I'll report back.

She flicked off the signal lamp and turned to Aleksy. They were going to be getting cozy again.

"I'm going back down, and we'll drop anchor. Then we're taking the Minersible out to get a closer look at the situation. Is that acceptable to you? If you'd prefer to stay here, I understand."

She braced herself for a rejection. His newfound ease in her presence didn't mean he wanted to put himself back into a situation where he couldn't avoid touching her. Operating the Minersible's arms would be easier if she had a partner to pedal and steer, but she would do it on her own if necessary.

His blue-gray gaze drove into her with an intensity that made her breath hitch.

"I wouldn't want to miss an opportunity for an adventure with you, Captain."

Was she imagining things, or was his voice unnaturally husky right now? Hell and damnation. This was going to be interesting.

Chapter 13

Captain's Log, 30 June, 1892
It is the duty of every good sailor to come to the aid of a
vessel in distress so long as such a rescue does not put her
own crew and passengers in excessive danger.

"My life was boring, once," Aleksy remarked. "I used to fear my whole life might consist of sweeping floors and hauling equipment. Now I'm helping pirates."

He eased up on his pedaling as the submersible approached the giant claw. The enormous contraption was over ten feet high and equally as wide. How were they supposed to free it with their tiny vehicle?

Nemo turned a wheel to extend the Minersible's much smaller claw arm. "Is this better or worse than being bored?"

He glanced at her, noting where their arms and thighs touched. His skin heated. "Better."

"I'm glad. Let's circle around the claw and see if we can find where it's jammed. I'll turn up our lights for a better look."

Aleksy pedaled harder and steered the submersible into a new trajectory. The small underwater boat was slower to respond than a bicycle, but he was growing accustomed to the simple controls. He took them into a slow arc around the claw and the shipwreck, letting Nemo do most of the watching.

"There," she said, using the boat's arm to point. "It looks like that piece of the claw isn't clamping on the ruined train car, but something underneath. Maybe it hooked on a section of rock. Pedal closer and I'll set us down on the ground."

Aleksy complied, and soon the Minersible bumped down on the lakebed. He relaxed his grip on the handlebars and leaned toward the window for a closer look.

"That's not a rock."

Nemo turned something on the control panel, and the arm banged against the ground, right where the big claw was stuck. A sonorous *tong* rolled through the water.

"Metal." She touched another control and the arm retracted into the submersible. "There's more wreckage here than what was visible on the surface."

"Why would a train car be sunk beneath the lake at all?" Aleksy wondered.

"Being carried across the lake on a barge, I suspect. To save taking the railroad all the way around the bottom of the lake and up into Wisconsin. Look at all the wooden bits strewn around. They must have hit quite the storm to tear the boat apart like that. The metal train cars fared somewhat better."

A second arm extended from the Minersible. A round blade with sharp, wicked-looking teeth jutted from the end. Nemo aimed the blade at the ground.

"I'm going to slice away a piece of whatever it is beneath the sand. It should free Merriman's claw contraption." She flicked a switch and the blade spun into a blur of terror, emitting a high-pitched whine as it tore through the corroded metal beneath it.

Aleksy jerked back as much as he was able in the small space. "My God, that saw is a nightmare! Why do you have such a thing?"

The captain smiled her self-possessed smile. "I installed a slicer in the event I needed to cut out a piece of something for a sample or to remove an obstruction."

"I guess this is an obstruction." He cringed. "But the noise!"

"It would be much worse if it weren't dampened by the wat—" She scrambled to turn the slicer off as the frozen claw popped free, flinging a sheared-off chunk of metal past the Minersible's bow. "Hard reverse!"

Aleksy shoved on the forward/reverse lever and pedaled furiously, sending the Minersible skittering away as the claw began to rise from the ground, taking the twisted remains of the train car with it. Bits of loose wood and rusty metal tumbled through the water. He cringed when a chunk of debris struck them, but the thick glass held fast.

Nemo mopped her brow with her sleeve. "Well, that was exciting." Her eyes flicked upward to where the wreckage and the claw were disappearing into the sailing ship. "I wonder if Merriman would tell me about his special ship and its secret false bottom. It must be a marvel of engineering."

Her wistful tone sent a stab of jealousy through Aleksy.

Really, Szekalski? Jealous of a pirate? The man is a criminal.

But also rich, smart, charming, and knowledgeable about both seafaring and engineering. He and Nemo had a great deal in common.

"Shall we see what's left behind before we return to the *Narwhal*?" Nemo asked, bringing Aleksy out of his thoughts.

They maneuvered the Minersible around the area, shining her lights down at the lakebed. Sand and splintered pieces of wood covered most of the ground, but here and there rust-pocked metal stood out among the wreckage.

Aleksy pedaled toward the hole left behind where the claw had been caught.

"Do you think that's another broken train car?" he asked.

Nemo lowered the craft to the ground. "Could be. Let's take a look inside." She adjusted the headlights to point down the hole. The beams glinted off a shiny surface inside.

Aleksy squinted at the reflection. "That's not steel."

"No. A mirror, perhaps? Or something made of glass? I'll try reaching inside and grabbing whatever it is."

The arm with the grabber again extended from their boat. Nemo aimed it at the hole, pushing it inside. Her mouth twisted into a frown of concentration as she worked.

"Got something!" she declared a moment later.

The arm retracted, carrying its prize: a cluster of rectangular bars, each over half a foot long and a few inches wide. Light danced off their lustrous surface.

Aleksy swore.

The grabber arm wobbled. "Gold," Nemo gasped. She reeled in the arm. A *thunk* below them told Aleksy the gold had been deposited into the small cargo compartment.

Nemo's eyes gleamed as brightly as the treasure she'd discovered. "I'm going back for more." The arm shot out again, and she hauled in a second pile, then a third.

"How much more do you think is down there?" Aleksy breathed.

"Quite a lot, I'd guess." She released the controls and twisted to look at him. "Enough to fund my research for a long time. I—" Her voice hitched. "I won't need to beg for a patron or work another job."

Her entire body vibrated with excitement. The smile on her face outshone any gold. Good Lord, was she beautiful. He'd help pirates every day, if it meant he could see her smile like this.

"I'm so happy for you," he murmured.

"Thank you." She leaned toward him, her chin tilting up and her lips parting.

This time, Aleksy didn't hesitate. He pressed his lips to hers and wrapped her in a fierce embrace.

Nisha melted into him. Her arms wound around his neck as their tongues tangled. She was sweet, hot, glorious. Every movement of her lips sent blasts of white-hot desire straight to his groin. He clutched her tighter and deepened the kiss.

When she made a little mewl of pleasure, he redoubled his efforts. He licked and explored her mouth, his hands beginning to wander, stroking down to her hips and buttocks. She arched against him, crushing him against the wall behind him. He cursed the awkward position and the handlebars that prevented him from dragging her onto his lap.

"Aleksy," she panted, when they came up for air. "This is…"

Foolish? Improper? Wonderful?

Instead of finishing her thought, she kissed him again, her mouth ravenous against his. Her fingers threaded through his hair, and she shifted to bring their bodies closer yet. Her wriggling rubbed her breasts against his chest, and he let out a muffled groan.

God, he needed more. He needed everything she would offer. He tried to turn in his seat, to give them more room, but his arm collided with the control panel and a switch dug painfully into his arm.

"Ow!" he yelped, at the same time the Minersible lurched.

Nisha drew back. "*Phew.*" She placed a hand on the lever that would lift them up toward the submarine. "Maybe this isn't the place."

"No," Aleksy agreed. "And we should, um, do something about the gold first?"

She nodded. "I don't think I'll be able to carry it all on the *Narwhal*. The weight could become an issue. But we should return to the ship. I want to signal to Merriman before he leaves."

Aleksy blinked. "The pirate? Why?" Was his brain fogged from the kiss? She'd done her favor. What was left to say?

This time, Nisha's grin was impish. "I'm going to make him an offer he can't resist."

Chapter 14

Captain's Log, 30 June, 1892
Have invited Captain Merriman of the SS Audacity *for a visit and consultation.*

"Have a seat." Aleksy jabbed the chef's knife in the direction of the table.

Merriman's eyebrows lifted and his mouth curved into a tiny smirk. "You know how to use that weapon in your hand?"

Aleksy grabbed an apple. The knife flashed in lightning-quick strokes, leaving a pile of neat, even wedges.

Merriman chuckled. "Touche."

Aleksy chopped up another apple, then dumped all the pieces onto a plate, alongside the slices of cheese he'd cut. Offering refreshments to their "guest" was all a pretense, of course. Aleksy had no desire to feed Merriman. But this was Nemo's ship and she'd decided to bring him on board. Since Aleksy trusted the pirate about as far as he could piss, he'd decided on a course of action that allowed him to keep a knife in his hand.

Merriman sat at the table, in Aleksy's usual spot. Nemo slid into her own seat across from him. Aleksy carried the plate of snacks over, bringing the knife with him. He took a seat beside Nemo, perching on the edge of the bench in case he needed to spring to his feet. He set the knife down in front of him and pushed the plate toward Merriman.

The pirate selected an apple slice and chewed slowly, his gaze wandering the room as he ate. A greedy gleam stole into his eyes.

"This is quite the machine," he said, eyeing the pipes running along the ceiling. "I'd love to learn how she works."

"Perhaps another day," Nemo replied. Her smile was wide, even though her clipped tone suggested, *when it's a cold day in hell.* "But tonight I think we ought to begin by talking about *your* ship."

"*Audacity*? She's a lovely little thing. Just what a man needs to carry his goods from port to port."

Little? And *his* goods? The pirate's ship was massive, and stuffed with plundered treasure. Though Aleksy admittedly couldn't complain about the latter, given the salvaged gold now sitting in the engine room.

"A lovely ship, indeed," Nemo replied. "I would enjoy seeing all her special innovations."

The pirate smirked. "Perhaps another day, Captain."

Aleksy chuckled. Maybe this meeting would go smoothly after all. The two captains clearly understood one another. He kept his hand resting beside the knife, regardless. If anything went wrong he would defend his lady.

The lady you'd like to have, he corrected himself. After that last kiss, it was difficult to think about anything else. If it weren't for the blasted pirate, maybe they'd be kissing again right now.

Nemo twirled an apple slice around in her fingers, but didn't bite into it. "I'm happy we were able to assist you tonight, Captain Merriman. I trust your cargo is safely on board? Did you find anything of value in the old train car?"

"Silver," the pirate confessed. "It was a fancy dining

car, once. Full of silver place settings and a handful of other saleable odds and ends. Much better to put it to use and earn money to feed my crew than leave it lost in the lake, don't you think?"

Nemo nodded. "You're finished here, then?"

Merriman hesitated a moment. "Yes. Why do you ask?"

Nemo popped the apple slice into her mouth and didn't reply until she'd washed it down with a drink from her flask. "I, too, have discovered something. I'm willing to share it, but my offer has strict conditions."

A speculative look crossed the pirate's face. Aleksy nibbled on a piece of cheese and studied the man. Merriman was a crafty, calculating sort of criminal. One who planned his capers and considered the consequences. That explained why Nemo had said he'd been "charged with piracy" rather than "convicted." Aleksy could hardly believe how boldly she was dealing with him. *She* was the one who ought to have a ship named *Audacity.*

"Tell me more," Merriman murmured, his voice husky, as if she'd offered a tryst rather than a business deal. If he made any attempt to touch her, Aleksy was stabbing him. No question about it.

Nemo relaxed in her seat, as if discussing the weather. "In the process of freeing your device, we found more wreckage beneath the sand. A boxcar, perhaps, or other type of cargo container. I want what's inside. At the moment, however, I have neither the time nor the necessary storage to haul it all away."

Merriman reached into his pocket and Aleksy's hand jerked instinctively toward the knife. The pirate laughed, lifting a wooden toothpick and poking it between his front teeth.

"You're a twitchy lad, aren't you? Fear not. The lady is

safe with me." His attention returned to Nemo. "Where do I come into this picture, Captain? I can't imagine you want to sail off and leave me to dig up this mysterious cargo on my own?"

"I wish to hire your services," she answered. "You use your special ship to lift the cargo and sail it to Detroit. In return, I will pay you with a share of the goods."

"Hmm…" Merriman tapped the toothpick against his bottom lip. "I gather this cargo is valuable."

"It is. I'm willing to pay you twenty-five percent. I've heard you're a man who keeps his word. Is that true?"

Merriman grinned. "It is. But I'm also a man who rarely makes promises. Too risky."

"Thirty percent of the haul," Nemo bargained. "No more, no less. No running off to Escanaba thinking you can sell it off to fur trappers and copper barons."

"I'll do it. For half the loot."

"Hah!" Nemo retorted.

"What's to stop me from sinking this pretty ship of yours and taking *all* the cargo?"

"What's to stop *me* from hiding where you'll never find me until one day I pop up and shoot you with my torpedoes?"

Aleksy turned all his attention to selecting another piece of cheese to mask his startlement. This ship had no torpedoes. No weapons of any kind. God, this woman! If it wouldn't have ruined her negotiating, he would have stood up and applauded her bravado.

Merriman's laugh rumbled through the room. "Forty-five percent."

"Thirty-five," Nemo challenged.

"Forty."

Her hand shot out. "Deal."

Merriman took hold of her hand and they shook. "Nice

to do business with you." When he released her, he rose from his seat. "I should return to my ship, unless you'd like to change your mind about giving me a tour?"

"Not today, I'm afraid," Nemo said, though not as coldly as before.

"May I ask what the cargo is that I'll be transporting for you?"

Nemo rose, reached into her pocket, and pulled out a single gold bar. She tossed it on the table, where it lay gleaming in the electric light.

Merriman let out a whistle. "Hell and damnation, woman."

"Sixty percent for me, forty for you," Nemo reminded him.

The pirate took a step backward, then gave her a sweeping bow. "You play a fine game, Captain. It's been an honor." He turned away, strode to the hatch, and climbed from the submarine.

Aleksy stared at the open hatch. He picked up the knife and speared a slice of apple. "If he steals your gold, I'll stab him for you."

Nemo climbed up the ladder to poke her head out the hatch. A moment later, she dropped down. "He's on his dinghy. I'll close up and then we'll be off. I want to find a deeper area where we can set down for the night."

Aleksy glanced at his watch. Nearly quarter to four. The sun would be rising before long. His shoulders sagged with sudden weariness. What a night.

He ate a bit more of the apples and cheese, leaving the rest for breakfast. Or lunch, since he was likely to sleep until noon. Then he tidied up the rest of the kitchen, including washing and drying the knife. When he slipped it into place beside a paring knife, he contemplated all the places he could stash the smaller blade: up a sleeve, tucked into a boot, sewn into the lining of his jacket. This adventure was bringing out his warrior instincts.

With the kitchen clean, he went to the control room to assist with the navigation. Nemo sat slightly hunched, as if she too had run out of energy. Aleksy flexed his fingers, struggling against the urge to massage her shoulders and back. The kiss in the Minersible had left him with no doubt they both wanted more. But too much remained unspoken and he was tired. He didn't dare to presume she would welcome his touch.

"You were remarkable," he said instead, hoping to lift her spirits with his words.

She looked over her shoulder to give him a brief smile. "I was terrified," she admitted. "I was certain he would see right through me, or even attempt to seize my ship."

"I would have chopped him up like an apple," Aleksy vowed.

Her smile broadened, and she turned quickly back to her work. "For a man who loves animals, you are quite blood-thirsty when it comes to your own species."

"Humans make bonds, like a pack of wolves. I am biologically predisposed to protect myself and those close to me."

Her reply was a long time coming. "Thank you," she said softly. "It's good to have a friend at my back."

Aleksy stepped closer, taking his place at her side. Close, but not touching. Here if she wanted him.

They sailed on in silence for another forty-five minutes before she declared it time to drop anchor. Aleksy had seen the shutdown procedure enough times to assist with the anchor and the lights while she saw to the other controls.

Soon, the ship was quiet, only the tiny lights along the floor and ceiling left to illuminate their path.

"We should sleep while we can," Nemo suggested. "Tomorrow—today, I suppose—we'll return to our plan."

"Tak, jasne. Of course."

Damn the plan. Aleksy didn't want to leave, even if it *was* the most sensible course of action. He wanted time to discover what noises he could coax out of her. To taste new parts of her. To see if the compatibility they had when working would carry over into the bedroom.

"We'll talk more later," Nemo pronounced. Her pointed tone conveyed everything he needed to know. They would talk about their kisses. They would talk about "more."

"Yes. Good night, Captain. Sleep well."

He strode off toward his bunk, desire thrumming in his veins despite the late hour. How much of that "more" he would get over the next few days, he couldn't guess. But he'd take all of it. For tonight, however, he'd take his sinful thoughts off to bed.

The bunkroom had its own light, and he flicked it on to check on Nadia. The axolotl's healing limb looked nearly normal now. She swam to the side of the tank to peer at him.

"Yes, I've got food for you," he said. He opened one of the storage compartments, plucked a worm out of the jar he kept there, and dropped the annelid into the tank. Nadia pounced on it and began to eat.

Aleksy changed swiftly into his nightshirt, then ducked into the washroom to brush his teeth. By now, he knew exactly how far to turn the handle to keep the sink from spurting all over. Strange how in less than two weeks this floating metal tube had come to feel like a home.

He slipped into bed, pulling the blanket up over himself, expecting to fall easily to sleep. He didn't. Thoughts of

Nisha danced through his mind. Nisha kissing him with wild abandon. Nisha across the hall in her own bed, only a few steps away. Nisha detailing all the wicked things she wanted from him, in her cool, collected way.

He squirmed. Why did it feel so hot in here? The submarine maintained a constant temperature, no matter their depth. He was wearing the exact same nightshirt under the exact same blanket as usual.

It was only him. Him and his unceasing desire and his litany of sinful thoughts.

Aleksy hiked up his nightshirt and wrapped a hand around his stiffening cock. He was probably well on the road to hell, but he'd long ago accepted that sometimes his baser urges got the better of him. If he couldn't sleep and he couldn't stop thinking of her, he might as well provide himself a bit of relief.

He let the memory of their kiss replay in his mind as he pumped his fist in smooth, rhythmic strokes. The slide of her tongue against his. The perfect curve of her buttocks in his hands. The tips of her breasts caressing his chest.

More, more, more.

His stroking picked up pace as his imagination carried him to a place where their clothing would no longer be a barrier. Where he could feel her warm, smooth skin and sink into the welcoming wetness between her legs.

A rustle of fabric made him flinch. Was he being too loud?

His hand stilled momentarily. No, this noise came from further than his own bed. Her bed?

A soft, breathy noise accompanied another swish of sheets. A barely there, whispered, "Oh."

"Matko boska," he hissed. She was there, in her bed, quite likely doing the same thing he was.

His hand flew faster, tugging and squeezing. Could she hear the sounds of his movements? His quickened breath? The thumping of his heart? His head lolled to one side and his eyes squeezed closed. Tingles built at the base of his spine.

God, oh, God.

He was close, so damn close from the very idea of her touching herself, thinking of him, wanting him, wanting this.

When the climax overpowered him, he couldn't suppress a groan.

* * *

Sleep eluded Nemo. Maybe she'd simply been awake too long. Maybe it was the lingering anxious energy from a night of pirates and gold.

Maybe it's your obsessive thoughts about Aleksy Szekalski.

He'd been oddly charming, threatening Merriman with a kitchen knife. Sweetly protective. A person could easily be deceived into thinking he was nothing but a quiet scholar, with his books and microscope. Nemo knew better. Intelligence and a scientific bent didn't have to mean timid. Aleksy continued to prove himself the sort of man who would never let a villain harm an innocent.

Or a not-so-innocent, in her case. The thoughts running through her head every time she'd looked at him this evening had definitely been of the impure variety. Figuratively speaking, of course. Nisha didn't believe sex was actually impure, immoral, or in any way bad. Her parents, naturally, had counseled her that sexual pleasures were to be reserved for the marriage bed, but she believed that unnecessarily strict. Especially when men's dalliances were usually excused by society and women's never were. Challenging the proscribed roles of the sexes had always been a favorite pastime of hers.

She tugged up the hem of her nightgown. She could lull herself to sleep with a good orgasm. And since her mind seemed focused on sex and the handsome man across the hall, release should be swift and strong.

Nisha thought back to his hands on her, the taste of his lips, and the way he swirled his tongue into her mouth, eager for more. Her body answered with a throb between her legs and a growing wetness. She slid a finger through her folds, rubbing the slick fluid up and over her clitoris.

Yes. So good. She imagined Aleksy watching her as she parted and stroked herself and teased her sensitive nub.

Do it like this. Touch me just like this.

In her fantasy, his fingers would reach out to take the place of hers. Then he'd ease himself down between her legs and use his mouth on her.

Nisha released a soft sigh. She wanted to moan, but then he would hear her, and she didn't want to disturb him. He was probably already asleep.

A faint shuffling noise came from across the hall, accompanied by whispered words that might have been a curse. Perhaps he was awake after all.

Her ears pricked up while her finger rubbed rapid, desperate circles over her clit. She caught the creak of his bed, the rhythmic stroke of his hand. Oh, gods, they were in this together. Both so hungry, so frantic, so close to bursting with the wanting.

Her finger pressed harder, moved faster. She dragged her other hand along her inner thigh, then pushed two fingers inside her, pumping in and out, pushing her toward the edge.

A groan, clearly audible, sounded from beyond her curtained doorway as Aleksy hit his own peak.

Yes, oh, yes.

Nisha bucked against her hands, no longer caring about being still or quiet, only caring that she found that same sweet release. She let out the moan she'd been holding back, and the orgasm swept over her, long and luxurious. She let herself revel in the sensation before blowing out a heavy, weary breath of satisfaction.

Aleksy cursed again, clearly this time. One of these days, she would have to ask him what the words meant.

"Sleep well," she called out.

She burrowed into her pillow. Tomorrow's breakfast would include quite the conversation.

Chapter 15

Captain's Log, 30 June, 1892
Is it really still June? All our overnight adventures have muddled my sense of time. No disruptions while we were sleeping.

Aleksy sang a bawdy sailing tune as he cracked eggs into a bowl.

"The moment we pulled into port, I spied the fairest miss. I said, 'Lass, I've been too long asea without a woman's kiss.'"

"Ooh, I don't know that one." Nemo strode into the room. She wore her usual green coveralls and had her hair tied back in a ponytail. Aleksy's pulse immediately sped up. He would always be drawn to her, whether in work clothes or the fanciest ballgown.

"I learned it on my voyage across the Atlantic," he explained. "It was the first time I added slang and innuendo to my academic and scientific English."

"That seems a fun way to learn. So does she kiss him?"

Aleksy sang the next few lines. "'You may not kiss me, sir,' she said. 'Begone and do make haste.' I said, 'I got a coin for you for but a little taste.' 'And another if you lift your skirts and let me have a peek.' She hoisted up her hem, spun 'round, and turned the other cheek."

Nemo burst out laughing. "Kiss my ass. That's what she said."

"Yes. The rest of the song has him spilling his ale, losing at cards, and stepping in excrement. Finally, he says he'd best return to the sea where he belongs." He poured the eggs into the frying pan, sprinkled in some cheese and chopped onions, and began to scramble it all together. "Would you like some eggs, Captain? It's not quite noon, so it can be breakfast or lunch."

"Brunch," Nemo replied. Aleksy had never heard that word, but he liked the sound of it. "And eggs will be perfect for brunch, thank you."

She sat down in her place at the table and popped one of the leftover apple slices into her mouth. They were brown this morning, but still tasty. Aleksy had already eaten two-thirds of them. He'd leave her the rest.

"I find it interesting that you eat eggs but not meat," she remarked.

"I don't like to harm animals. The hens don't mind laying eggs that will never grow a baby bird, so I don't mind eating them. But I wouldn't buy from a farmer who mistreated his chickens."

"That makes sense. I eat some meat, but no beef. And the animals must be raised and slaughtered in an ethical manner. Both my older sisters keep their families vegetarian as a religious practice. They don't eat eggs and only certain cheeses. But their reasons are similar to yours. Non-violence to other life forms is an important part of Hinduism."

Aleksy began to portion out the cooked eggs onto two plates. "Is that why you have no weapons on your submarine?"

"Yes. Fortunately, I have a heathen like you to defend me if any pirates become dangerous."

He carried the plates to the table and sat. "I am happy to be your champion. Although Catholics aren't supposed to kill people, either."

He scooped up a bite of his non-lethal brunch. Nemo was so easy to talk to. Food, family, religion, bawdy songs… conversation about anything simply flowed between them. No wonder they made such a good working team. No wonder the desire between them blazed so brightly.

"But I do admit to sometimes falling asleep in church," he added. He gave her a wide grin and a flirtatious twitch of the eyebrows. "I think we both know I occasionally stray from the rules."

Aleksy expected a grin, a laugh, a saucy retort. He got none of it. She sat still and silent, her expression void of emotion. Where was the woman from last night? It hadn't been his imagination when she'd let him hear her orgasm and then cheekily bid him goodnight. Currently, however, that side of her was locked so tightly away, it might as well have been nonexistent.

He tried to think up polite ways to apologize. Maybe she was embarrassed by her earlier brazenness. That didn't seem like her, but he wouldn't say it was impossible. Humans could be odd creatures when negotiating social and sexual situations.

Before he could conjure a good way to break the tension, she spoke.

"Your innuendo regarding last night's events brings us nicely to the matter we need to discuss." She ate a bite of eggs before continuing. "We were both caught unaware, I think, by this attraction between us."

Aleksy nodded around his own mouthful of food.

"It's undeniable, though, and it appears that we both feel compelled to act on it. Is that true?"

"It's true for me." He wanted her with an intensity he hadn't felt in a long time, if ever. What had begun as mere interest had grown into complete infatuation. She intrigued him, with her unconventional ways, her sharp mind, her daring, her poise, and the heated passions beneath. Her face was as pretty as any he'd ever seen—a biological reaction, perhaps, to their compatibility? It made sense to be stimulated by someone he could get on well with.

"Good," Nemo said. "Since we have that established, the next step is to rationally consider how to handle the matter. We have a number of options, and they each have their pros and cons."

"Do we need to make a chart?" Aleksy jested, hoping to draw out a smile and put her at ease.

You don't have to be the captain directing your crew. You can talk to me about this. You can talk to me about anything.

He kept those thoughts to himself. It was possible her dispassionate demeanor wasn't a cover for feelings of embarrassment or awkwardness, but simply because she wanted to be explicitly clear about the situation. Either way, he didn't want to unsettle her.

He gave her what he hoped was a friendly and encouraging smile. He missed the spontaneity of their kisses, but for now he would hear what she had to say. They could always return to normal afterward.

"Doing nothing will leave us frustrated," Nemo went on. "I dislike this option. If we're distracted by this, it could interfere with our ability to work and make us more likely to make a mistake that could alert the enemy to our presence. I think it's better to alleviate our frustrations, even though we have only a few days remaining together."

The forkful of eggs he'd just eaten settled like a stone

in his stomach. A few days wasn't enough time. A few days would barely give him time to begin.

It's better than nothing.

Nemo pushed her eggs around on her plate, looking off into the distance. "The second option would be to continue as we were last night. It's simple, has no potential complications, and requires little planning. But I'm not certain it would achieve the desired goal. Speaking for myself, I would still desire to touch you."

She returned to her brunch, as if she hadn't just sent a bolt of lightning straight to his cock. Hell, yes, she could touch him. Everywhere. For as long as she liked.

"I… would also desire that." God, he *sounded* aroused. Couldn't they skip the rest of this discussion and get to the sex? "And I would wish to touch you as well."

"Which leaves us with option 3: indulge ourselves."

"Yes, please." He shoveled more eggs into his mouth, eager to get this meal over with so he could taste Nisha instead.

"This is where we run into possible consequences," she elaborated. "I don't have any sort of contraception on board. I, therefore, have certain rules about what we can and cannot do. I am willing to exchange pleasures using hands and mouths, but there will be no intercourse. Not even if you intend to withdraw. If that is acceptable to you, we can proceed."

Aleksy gulped down his food. "It is acceptable." As much as he wanted to know how it would feel to be inside her, he entirely understood and respected her reasons. He'd enjoy whatever she had to offer.

"Excellent. After brunch, we need to sail into deeper waters to ensure we will be well and truly hidden for the next few days. We can begin this new phase of our relationship at bedtime. We will use my bed, which is large enough to accommodate us both. Feel free to join me in my room when you're ready. It's probably easiest if you arrive naked, but if you prefer to wear your nightshirt and remove it once in the room, I understand."

He blinked, suddenly uncertain. They were to have a specific time? And a… procedure? What had happened to giving in to their urges in a sudden, passionate kiss? It made much more sense to him to let it all happen naturally.

But, again, he'd promised to go along with her wishes. He'd wait until bedtime. It would be fine.

* * *

The day had gone smoothly. Nemo had navigated the *Narwhal* into an area of the lake one hundred fathoms deep. She'd gotten some excellent data to begin her Lake Michigan map. Aleksy had taken a number of samples and spent hours with his microscope.

Had he discovered anything interesting? He'd been quiet today. No rushing into her control room with news. No excited exclamations or frantic searches through her library. Perhaps he'd grown tired of the routine.

Nisha scrubbed her hands and splashed cool water on her face. He probably wanted off this boat. Here she was, in her nicely-sized cabin, with her own personal washbasin, a writing desk, and a bed wide enough for two. He remained stuck in a narrow crew bunk, with barely room to change clothes. She could picture him dancing with glee the moment he set foot on shore.

She spun away from the sink. This wasn't the time to be thinking of such things. In minutes, Aleksy would be joining her. Easing the desires that had been plaguing them. That was the only thing that ought to be on her mind.

Nisha stripped slowly, hanging her coveralls on a peg and tossing her underthings into a container with other items needing laundering. She snatched her nightgown off another peg and pulled it over her head.

Shouldn't you be sprawling on the bed, naked, ready to lure him in like the world's most skilled temptress?

She didn't feel like a temptress, though. Her usual bedtime ritual had been disrupted. When she ought to have been crawling under the sheets and closing her eyes, instead she was left waiting. Uncertain.

She sat on the edge of the bed, then flopped backward and stared up at the ceiling. Her gaze followed the conduit pipe that protected the delicate wiring for the ship's electrical components. Then one for compressed air. Water. Steam. The arteries of the *Narwhal*, carrying life-sustaining elements to every part of her body.

A hollow knock echoed off the wall outside her door, shaking her from her preoccupation. She sat up quickly.

"Come in."

Aleksy parted the curtain and stepped through. Like her, he'd put on his nightclothes. The shirt hung down past his knees, but his feet were bare beneath. The neckline hung open in a V deep enough to reveal a hint of dark hairs on his chest.

He clasped his hands behind his back. "Good evening."

"Good evening. How is your axolotl?" Not the enticing, sensual opening she probably ought to have tried, but it was the question that had first sprung to mind. Did he feed his pet before bed? Play with her?

"She's well. You are welcome to visit her at any time. She enjoys the attention." His eyes darted back and forth. "This is a nice room."

"Thank you. I'm sorry yours is so small."

He shrugged. "I am tough."

Nisha shifted to her left. She needed to stop this meaningless chatter. Aleksy had joined her here for a purpose. "Would you like to sit down?"

He sat, but didn't touch her. Blast it all, why was this so awkward? She'd tried to make it as simple as possible: two people, a bed, no distractions. She turned her head and kissed him. Maybe action would work better than words.

Aleksy grasped her around the waist and dragged her fully onto the bed, dropping down beside her. He brought one hand around to her breast and squeezed.

"Lights on or off?" he asked. "Clothes on or off?"

"Uh…" This was supposed to be easy. Why was it not easy? Nisha tried to distract herself by running her hands over his torso. "This is fine."

His muscles were hard and strong beneath the linen of his nightshirt. How long had he been doing manual labor for Stromberg? Years? Did he miss having physical things to do?

A tickle ran up her thigh as his fingers delved beneath her nightgown. Her attention drifted back to the here and now. She enjoyed his touch, had been craving it for days. She only needed to quiet her over-busy mind and let herself relax into the moment.

Nisha closed her eyes and focused on her breathing, trying to clear her head. Aleksy's hand pushed up between her legs, spreading her open to his touch. He stroked gently, but her body wasn't responding as quickly as she might have liked, and she winced at the lack of moisture.

Aleksy paused, licked his finger, and rubbed the newly lubricated digit across her clitoris. Better. Nice.

Her mind floated away again, wondering what he'd been doing all day, during those hours they hadn't spoken. Was he bored? Did he like the books he'd taken from her library? What did he read for fun at home?

She shifted when his explorations hit a not-exactly comfortable spot. She ought to move his hand a little bit. And touch him. She'd entirely forgotten to keep touching him.

This wasn't working. Her head was in the clouds. Their physical interactions lacked the explosive heat that had always been between them before. It would take her hours to climax like this.

"Wait."

He pulled his hand away and sat up. "Would you like me to try something different?"

No.

The answer formed immediately in her mind. She *could* keep going. It wouldn't be difficult to find a suitable lubricant. If she truly wanted him, here and now, she would happily be taking the necessary steps to bring them both pleasure.

No, the problem was that she *didn't* want this, and she didn't quite understand why. But the spark between them was missing. Her mind wasn't in it. Her heart wasn't in it.

"No, thank you," she finally replied. "I think tonight isn't our night."

Honestly, she would be perfectly content to go back to talking about his axolotl and wondering whether he missed any part of his old job. She wanted to know if he would stare into a microscope all day every day if he had any other choice. Would it be weird if she asked him to stay and talk to her, instead?

Yes. Yes, it would be.

Aleksy pushed himself up off the bed and straightened his nightshirt. "That's fine. I won't bother you any longer. Sleep well."

"Good night."

He lifted the curtain and ducked out.

Nemo cursed softly. "You well and truly bungled that, Nisha Majhi," she murmured.

She was an engineer. Solving problems was her life. Why, in this, was she entirely at a loss for what to do?

It's only a few more days. Then he'll be gone and you won't even have a problem anymore.

Not a comforting thought.

Chapter 16

Captain's Log, 1 July, 1892
Exploring below 100 fathoms. Continued progress on map
and sample gathering.

Aleksy found Nemo cleaning up after her breakfast when he stepped into the kitchen. She turned when she heard his footsteps and gave him a fond smile. A rush of relief washed over him. Part of him had been convinced she'd blamed him for their inelegant parting last night.

"Good morning," she said. "Did you sleep well?"

"Fine, thank you."

Liar. He'd slept fitfully, suffering from a different kind of frustration than the one that had previously haunted him. He was running out of time to investigate the passion between them, but it was clearly something that couldn't be forced. He didn't want to miss his opportunity. He didn't want *her* to miss the opportunity. She deserved unrestrained, explosive pleasure, and he wanted to be the one to provide it.

Aleksy opened the icebox and peered at the food inside. The ingenious device used cold lake water to cool the interior when ice wasn't available. It could safely store fresh food for days.

"I'm sorry about last night." Nemo's voice behind him

made him jump. He'd expected her to head right for the control room. "I wasn't feeling amorous."

Aleksy grabbed a chunk of cheese and an oblong bread roll. Neither strictly needed to be kept in the icebox, but it was spacious and kept mold away. He turned to face Nisha, nudging the door closed with his elbow.

"There's no need to apologize. Your feelings are always valid. And I don't think many people can be in the mood for such activities every night. I wasn't particularly excited, myself."

"Ah." A tiny flush gave her cheeks a hint of a copper sheen. "We can arrange to try again at another time, as long as you're still interested."

He didn't nod and didn't say yes. But he did make a vague sound of assent around the mouthful of cheese he'd bitten off. Nemo could interpret it however she liked. What he meant was, "Yes, I'm very much interested, but there aren't going to be any more arrangements."

He knew what the problem was. The pattern was there to see in their kisses. Their first time had to be unplanned. Impulsive, even. Anything else wouldn't work for him, and he doubted it would work for her, either. Starting right now, they would be doing things his way.

He wouldn't challenge her authority as captain or insist on making decisions for her, though. That wasn't his way, either. His way was more subtle. More gradual. And, hopefully, a damned lot of fun.

Aleksy Szekalski was going a-courting.

* * *

Aleksy took care not to let his finger slip from where it marked his page as he waved his book at Nemo.

"Guess what I found!"

She looked up from the controls. "A map to more lost gold?"

"A whole page about axolotls," he replied. He opened the book to give her a look. "The diagram is beautiful. It looks just like Nadia."

"It does." She ran a finger down the page. "Habitat, diet, behavior. Oh! And a large section about their mysterious regenerative abilities." She laughed. "This is a rather long-winded way to say, 'we have no idea how this works.'"

"Isn't it? An excellent reference, though. I'm going to borrow the next few volumes, if you don't mind."

Her grin lit her face. *Yes.* That was the Nisha he wanted to see. The scientist so eager to discover new things she'd built herself an underwater boat.

"Please take them," she said. "I love to see you reading my books. I can't possibly read through them all myself, but I wanted a fully stocked library so I could look things up."

"Wonderful. Thank you. I'll be back if I discover anything else interesting."

Her smile followed him all the way out of the room. Oh, yes, he would be back. Again and again, making her smile and laugh. He would share every bit of excitement he could conjure until she flung herself into his arms, longing for excitement of another kind.

Aleksy skimmed the next volume, found more fun facts, then set about preparing lunch. Food was a traditional tool of wooing, even among non-humans. He would win himself a mate via sustenance and science.

Nisha wafted into the room before he had even finished, drawn by the aroma of the meal simmering in the pot. His own nose tingled from the intriguing scent of unfamiliar spices.

"You heated up one of my Indian dishes!" she exclaimed. "And here I thought you were afraid to try them."

Aleksy gave the food a final stir, then turned off the heat. "I am. They seem spicy. I don't usually eat spicy. But I want to try the things you eat with your family. If we were in my neighborhood I would feed you all the things, starting with kapusta and pierogi."

One dark eyebrow lifted. "I have no idea what those are."

"Then it's fair, because I don't know what your spicy chickpea soup is, either."

"It's called cholar dal. My mother makes many varieties of dal, and you ought to try them all. Eventually you'll stop turning red in the face from the heat. Grab some bread. It will help cut the spice."

Aleksy poured the dal into a pair of bowls, then joined her at the table. The food was spicy enough to make him sweat, but it was also delicious, and Nemo had been right about the bread helping. Though he didn't truly need it. Her happiness at sharing part of her heritage with him was worth a mountain of spices.

"You really are turning red," she remarked, eyes twinkling. "But you've nearly cleaned your bowl already. My mother would be pleased."

"I'm happy to please." He gave her a playful wink and reached for the book that lay open nearby. "And now that I have enticed you with food…" He let the sentence hang for a moment, giving the word "enticed" time to settle in. "I will further thrill you with this brilliantly comprehensive chapter on cephalopods. I'm sorry, but we don't know any freshwater cephalopods. We are unlikely to see one here in the lake."

"Maybe they hide in the deep waters. Maybe you'll discover one, like you discovered that tiny shrimp."

The very idea made his heart beat faster, no matter how improbable it was. Maybe someday he could go to the ocean with her and find a new species of octopus.

You are leaving in two days.

"An octopus does not have tentacles," he said, defiantly returning to his courtship-by-science. "It has eight arms. A squid has eight arms and two tentacles."

"What's the difference?"

"Suction." Once again, Aleksy paused to give her plenty of time to consider the innuendo. It also gave him time to contemplate all the places he'd love to apply suction to her. Lips. Neck. The curve of her breasts where they swelled from her corset. The inside of her thigh.

Nisha coughed. "And?"

He blinked. "Przepraszam. Sorry. Arms have suckers all the way down. But tentacles only have suckers on the club-shaped tips." He pushed the book across the table so she could see the diagrams.

"Interesting."

"There's much more. They can propel themselves by shooting jets of water. They can spray ink to confuse enemies. They can change colors to match their environment." The words picked up speed as he went, tumbling out uncontrollably. "They have three hearts. They can be very, very smart, and some octopuses in captivity have tricked their handlers. The nautilus is unusual now because it has a shell, but we have many fossils of extinct cephalopod shells. They do not have long lifespans, but we believe even the giant squid can grow to full size in only a few years." His hand shot out to flip the page. "There's a whole page on the giant squid. Can you believe they can be forty feet long? I would love to see one for myself. They live in cold, deep ocean water. Do you think we could find one someday in your submarine?"

Nemo had both elbows on the table, leaning over the book. "I would love to see one."

"The suction cups on their arms and tentacles can be up to two inches in diameter! Can you imagine how powerful its grip must be? No wonder there are tales of creatures rising up from the depths to sink ships!" He rocked back in his seat, suddenly winded from the flurry of words. "Am I talking too much?"

"No," she answered without the slightest hesitation. "You're talking precisely enough."

Heat bloomed in his cheeks, and he hoped it would appear to be nothing more than the lingering effects of the spicy food. His fascination with all things biological ran wild on occasion. Nisha didn't seem to mind, however. In fact, she was looking at him with a soft, perhaps even tender, expression. As if she found him charming.

He started to reach for her, but she had already begun to rise from her seat. "I have to return to the helm, but I'll make a note about cephalopods for potential oceanic research. Come see me when you find more interesting sea life and we can add them to the list."

She picked up her empty bowl, but he waved for her to put it down. "I'll clean up."

Her tender smile grew a tiny bit broader. "Thank you."

Aleksy nodded. He admired her stride as she crossed the room. Confident. Relaxed. His science was working. She liked his information, and she became excited when he was excited. Next time he had to be close to her. The times they'd kissed, they'd been both excited and nearly touching. Maybe he could hold the book while showing her a particularly interesting page.

He washed and stowed the dishes, then returned to the table, where the book still lay open to the section about cephalopods. At the very bottom of the page, beyond where he had read earlier, a subheading said, "Mating Habits." He grasped the corner of the page and turned it carefully.

Fascinating. No diagrams, but a few key phrases started ideas dancing around in his head. He could definitely use this. As soon as he got close to her, he would unleash his newfound knowledge.

Science was fun.

Chapter 17

Captain's Log, 1 July, 1892
Emergency systems in working order.

Each time Aleksy entered the control room with a new tidbit of information, Nemo's heart made an extra thump of pleasure. Maybe it was silly, but she loved listening to him rave about the things that caught his interest. There was so much pure joy in it. Her dearest friends shared a similar fervor for knowledge, as did her grandmother, who had always been her biggest champion. Adding a new person to that select group was a rare and special treat.

Nemo brought the ship to a halt to perform an extra set of measurements and samples. She'd traveled a shorter distance today than originally planned, but more time gathering data and less time piloting was exactly what she needed. Today, she felt back on track. Doing what she was meant to do.

Footsteps behind her made her turn. Aleksy bounded into the room, two thick books in his arms. Scraps of paper jutted from between the pages, marking points of interest.

The smile he gave her made her breath catch. It was full of good cheer, but with the slightest crooked hitch, as if he'd suddenly had a wicked thought. He didn't leer, didn't ogle, yet his intent gaze gleamed with barely restrained desire.

Potential energy. Ready and waiting.

"What would you like to hear about this time?" he asked, striding toward her. "Shark anatomy? The sea turtle lifespan? Or…" His lips twitched and his eyebrows lifted in an expression of gleeful mischief. "I could tell you all the things I missed about cephalopods."

That sentence should not have made her skin heat and her limbs twitch. It should not have made her rise from her chair and step toward him. And it certainly should not have made her lick her lips in anticipation of a kiss.

"What about the cephalopods?"

"I could talk about their beaks and the way they feed." He moved toward her, slowly closing the gap between them as he spoke. "Or about their blue blood. But I think…" He stopped, not near enough to kiss her, but near enough to reach out and touch her. His voice dropped to a husky whisper. "You want to hear about their mating habits."

"Yes." Nisha closed the remaining space between them. This was what had been missing last night, for both of them. Perhaps it was something that couldn't be summoned on command. It didn't fit neatly into any plan, this way, but she *was* an explorer, after all. She had to be prepared for anything. "Tell me."

"When octopuses mate," Aleksy murmured, "they wrap their many arms around each other and press together." His arms encircled her, as if demonstrating. "Sometimes, they are mouth-to-mouth." He brushed his lips over hers. "And sometimes, the male will put his mouth to the female's neck."

He shifted slightly, then bent to kiss her neck. Nisha tilted her head for a better angle. She clasped him tightly around the waist.

"So many arms." His hands began to wander. "So much suction."

He sucked the skin of her neck, and pleasure zinged up

and down her spine. She let out a delighted gasp as his lips and tongue continued a leisurely perusal of the column of her throat.

"Maybe we should—" Nisha lost her train of thought when Aleksy's lips closed over her earlobe. "Maybe—"

Her brain refused to function. How had she not known she was ticklish there? His gentle suction started a vibration radiating from the soft cartilage of her ear to every nerve in her body.

"A bed?" she suggested, still unable to form complete sentences.

He made a soft noise against her ear, but she couldn't tell if it was a yes, a no, or simply an expression of his own pleasure. His hands had found their way to the buttons of her boiler suit, popping them open, one by one. As he moved further, easing open the fabric that shielded her breasts, her nipples tightened beneath her corset.

"To hell with the bed," she muttered. She turned her head, cupped Aleksy's face in her hands, and kissed him with everything she had.

The inarticulate groan he released was all the proof she needed that she'd made the right decision. Whatever this was between them—animal magnetism, primal lust, some reaction to continued close proximity—it was potent. He tasted better than a well-aged whiskey, but caused an equally intense fire in her belly.

The coveralls slipped from her shoulders, and she released Aleksy long enough to wriggle free and let the garment pool around her ankles. Nisha sucked in a breath and popped open the clasps of her corset. It fell to the floor, leaving her in only her combinations, her dark nipples clearly visible through the thin layer of fabric.

He stared at her for a long moment. "Jesteś taka piękna," he breathed.

She needed no translation. The stark hunger in his eyes and the bulge in his trousers said all she needed to know. A pink flush had crept over his neck and cheeks, and his chest rose and fell in breaths a touch more rapid than usual. She wasn't any more exposed than she'd been last night. How could everything be so entirely different?

Aleksy gently cupped his hands around her breasts. "How do you want me to touch you?"

Even that soft pressure was enough to send a new rush of arousal straight to her core. "Just touch," she gasped, once again finding it difficult to keep her thoughts in order. "Anywhere. Everywhere."

He caught her mouth in a drugging kiss as he squeezed her breasts and teased her nipples with light pinches. Nisha leaned into his caresses, dragging her own hands over his chest and back.

Yes, yes. This was what she'd wanted. What she'd known could be between them. Kisses that shorted some wire in her brain. Hands that made her body burn for more.

She seized one of his hands to guide it between her legs, but instead of obliging her, he grasped her about the waist and lifted her up to sit atop the control panel. Then he knelt in front of her and began unlacing her right boot.

"It will be better if we get this all the way off," he explained, giving a tug on her suit, where it tucked into the top of her boot.

"Yes," she agreed. She was near to panting with longing for him. The delay ought to have frustrated her. Instead, the sight of his fingers working her laces caused an upwelling of affection. He was kind and thoughtful, undressing her with care and perhaps even devotion.

He cast aside one boot, then the other, then tugged the coveralls fully off. Nudging her legs apart, he fitted himself between her thighs, then spread open her combinations to expose her to his view.

"Jesteś piękna," he repeated, then asked, "Are you comfortable?"

Nisha squirmed, every cell in her body clamoring to feel his fingers and lips on her. "Yes. Please."

The stroke of his tongue was like velvet on her sensitive flesh. He took his time tasting her, making small noises of enjoyment that caused her to moan in response. Every lick and suck sent a new wave of delight pulsating through her. She splayed out her hands to brace herself, not caring that the switches and dials dug into her palms. No pain mattered when in the throes of such bliss. Aleksy lavished attention on her clit, teasing it with little swirls of his tongue, then sucking until her back arched and she thrust against his mouth.

"Oh. Oh, gods, I—"

It was too much. The pressure was too much, and she was going to collapse under it, crushed from the unstoppable force of his ministrations.

He gave a final flick of his tongue, and she broke, her entire body spasming in ecstatic relief. She clawed at the metal beneath her hands, trying to anchor herself as pleasure spun around and through her.

Alarms began to blare. Lights flashed red and yellow. Aleksy fell back in surprise. Nisha could only blink. What was happening?

Several seconds passed before the incessant *ah-ooh-ga* of the klaxon horn jolted her from her post-coital haze. The ship!

Nemo hopped down from her perch, whirled around,

and began setting things to rights. In her distracted state, she'd flipped several switches, some of which weren't intended for use at the same time. Fortunately, she'd added the alarm to prevent any catastrophe. Within moments, she had everything as it should be. The noise ceased and the lights stopped flashing.

She turned. Aleksy had risen to his feet and stood watching her, his cheeks still flushed with arousal. Their eyes locked, and they stared at one another in silence.

A sudden grin spread across his face. Giddiness burbled up inside her. They burst into simultaneous laughter, falling into each other's arms and laughing until tears of mirth ran down their cheeks.

Just when Nisha had managed to catch her breath, Aleksy said, "It's good to know your orgasm detector is working."

She dissolved once more into helpless giggles. Together, they stumbled toward her bedroom to continue their activities, the sounds of their merriment ringing from the sub's metal walls.

Chapter 18

Captain's Log, 4 July, 1892
Happy Independence Day?

Nisha took her time pleasuring Aleksy, in retaliation for the delicious orgasm he'd just given her. He was getting close now, squirming and muttering semi-incoherent swears. She loved seeing him like this. The last few days had been a pure delight. They'd meandered through Lake Michigan, pausing at random intervals for research and spontaneous lovemaking.

She sucked harder and he hit his climax, letting out a prolonged groan. Excellent. He'd definitely enjoyed that.

Nisha climbed off Aleksy to lay beside him. He hooked an arm around her, pulling her snugly against him. This part was always wonderful. His fingertips brushed over her skin, soft and soothing. He pressed a kiss to her brow. Nestled against his warmth, with her body relaxed, the whole world seemed at peace. If these minutes turned into hours, she wouldn't protest.

She twisted, turning her face into the pillow as hot tears abruptly stung her eyes. This morning would be their last time. The moment they left this bed they would begin preparations for their separation. The *Narwhal* would surface and sail into the harbor at Port Washington, Wisconsin, and there Nisha and Aleksy would part ways, possibly forever.

She forced herself to breathe normally, even as the pillow grew damp beneath her. She wouldn't ruin this for him. Wouldn't upset him with her heartache. Aleksy deserved to step off this vessel happy and free, safe from Stromberg and ready to start fresh. Nisha had no doubts that he'd find a path to success. He was brilliant and kind. Anyone decent would support him in his journey.

As she would. It didn't matter that her entire body was screaming to cling to him and never let go. Nor did it matter that she was ninety-nine point nine percent certain she'd fallen irrevocably in love with him. She had no right to keep him here, and above all she wanted him healthy and happy. Even if she never saw it with her own eyes.

"Nisha?"

She flinched.

"I'm sorry," he added hurriedly. "Did you fall asleep? You were unusually still. I didn't mean to wake you."

"I wasn't asleep." She rubbed her face into the pillow, drying away the last of the tears. "I was only thinking. We have a lot to do today."

"Oh. Yes."

He pulled away, and a new pang of sorrow stabbed into Nisha's chest.

This is how it has to be. This is the right decision.

She scurried off the bed and began to dress, doing her best not to look at him. Everything would be fine, if she controlled her breathing and let her body relax. She was the imperturbable Captain Nemo. Nothing would keep her down.

Breakfast was quick, with neither of them saying much. Nisha avoided prolonged eye contact, lest her emotions get the better of her again. She had a job to do.

"It should only take an hour or so to bring us to the harbor and up to the surface," she informed Aleksy. "I trust that will give you time to pack."

He replied with a curt nod. "I will go do that."

Nemo hurried into the control room and threw herself into her work, checking and double-checking every gauge, and steering the ship with far greater precision than the open water required. She sank so completely into the task, she failed to notice she was no longer alone, until a *thud* sounded behind her.

She jumped and whirled around.

"I'm sorry." Aleksy glanced down at the suitcase sitting on the floor beside him. "I startled you again." For an instant, their gazes locked, and then he looked quickly down at the small specimen tank he held. The axolotl wriggled inside. "Nadia doesn't like the travel tank."

"Ah." Well, that made two of them who disliked this parting. Aleksy, on the other hand, looked ready to spring from the ship. He'd shaved, slicked down his hair, and donned a suit, complete with jacket and bow tie. No more shirtsleeves. No more slightly disheveled appearance. Gods, she missed him already and he was standing in the same room.

She cleared her throat and turned back to the controls. "You are right on time. We are only a half-dozen fathoms from the surface. You can watch out the window."

"That sounds enjoyable."

There was a slight clunk as he set Nadia's tank down, and a moment later he appeared at Nemo's side. He stood stiffly, looking straight ahead. Nemo did the same.

Remain calm. No making this maudlin.

As the ship rose higher, however, she couldn't help but steal a glance at him, trying to imprint him on her brain. She didn't linger, but a moment later she caught a slight turn of his head in her peripheral vision and felt his eyes on her. Had he noticed her staring? Had she revealed too much?

"Nearly there," she stated, making a smooth gesture at the top of the window, where a narrow shaft of sunlight appeared above the bobbing waves. Fretting now would be pointless. Aleksy was taking their separation in stride. He was clearly ready to leave. She wouldn't burden him with her sadness.

The *Narwhal* inched out of the water, exposing a cloudless sky and a day so bright Nemo had to squint.

Sunshine! Even through the window, the warmth of it on her face lightened her heart. They'd been too long in the darkness. Too long without fresh, open air. As marvelous as her submarine was, and as much as she loved the mysteries of the depths, she also needed the beauty of the surface.

A contented exhalation beside her caused her to glance Aleksy's direction. He wore a smile of unrestrained pleasure, not unlike the smile he graced her with after a vigorous romp in bed. Her heart leapt. If he could look at her that way, then maybe...

No. He's happy because we're surfacing. Because he's getting out of here.

His smile vanished. Almost in unison, they both jerked their heads back to stare out the window.

The *Narwhal* bounced in the waves as she achieved surface buoyancy. Ahead of them, the Wisconsin coastline spread across the horizon. The man-made harbor jutted out into the water, welcoming ships safely into port. Nemo's view of it was somewhat obstructed by a vessel that appeared to be heading directly toward the submarine.

She shielded her eyes from the light and squinted. "Dammit," she muttered, reaching for the switch to sound the *Narwhal's* horn. Even if that ship didn't have a proper lookout, they would at least hear her. Fortunately, there was enough room to maneuver and avoid any collision.

"Is that…" Aleksy leaned toward the window. "Kurwa!"

Nemo's eyes, still adjusting to the bright light, didn't immediately spot what had caused him to swear. When she saw it, her stomach turned over. A mauve stripe running the full length of the white ship. Stromberg.

"Shit, shit, shit!"

The ship wasn't making a leisurely trip out of the harbor, either. He was coming for them at full speed. A harsh glare flashed from something large and metallic at the ship's prow.

Nemo shoved the throttle and grabbed the wheel, turning her hard to starboard. The *Narwhal* was faster on the surface than submerged. Faster than Stromberg's steamship, with any luck. Only a narrow band near the shore was shallow here. If they could flee to deeper water, they could dive.

And then what? You hid before and he's here. Somehow, he tracked you the entire time.

"Keep watch on that ship," she blurted, as her hands moved feverishly over the controls.

Aleksy jabbed a finger toward the window, but she didn't have time to figure out what he was pointing at.

"There's a… a thing," he babbled. "A big… hook thing."

She spared a glance. From this angle, she could now see that the metal on the prow was an enormous harpoon gun, bigger even than those used on whaling ships. Instead of a barbed projectile, it had been loaded with a massive grappling hook.

"They're trying to catch us. Shit. At least they don't want to sink us. Hold tight. I'm going to show Stromberg that top speed he was so interested in."

Nemo pushed the *Narwhal* to her limits, but the distance

between the two ships continued to narrow. Dammit, why did watercraft have to turn so slowly?

"Fuck the laws of physics," she growled.

They were nearly parallel to the shoreline. A moment more and they could take off at full power. *Get away first, then get to deep water.*

"Nisha! Nisha!"

Aleksy's wild gesticulating almost blocked her view of the new threat. A second ship was bearing down on them from their starboard side. A familiar, wooden-hulled steamship, sitting low in the water, cutting off their path to freedom.

"The pirate!" Aleksy let out a long string of mixed English and Polish swears. "I knew it! I knew he couldn't be trusted!"

A wave of nausea swept over Nemo. No. It couldn't be. Merriman wouldn't betray her. She'd *liked* the charismatic criminal. They'd helped him! Shared the secret of the gold with him!

But she couldn't deny what lay before her eyes. They'd been flanked.

Chapter 19

Captain's Log, 4 July, 1892
See below for notes on unexpected speed and
maneuverability test.

I don't have to leave yet.

Aleksy almost smacked himself for that thought. They were on the verge of being reeled in like a fish. He ought to be trembling in terror. And he *was* afraid. But he couldn't deny that he also felt he'd been given a bit of a reprieve. For now, he and Nisha were still a team.

"How can I help?" He hoped Nisha had some idea, because he didn't.

She remained intent on the controls, steering the submarine through the painfully slow turn. "I'm taking us down. We'll have to try to pass under Merriman's ship."

"Under?" he gasped. "But…"

Nisha's face was a mask of concentration, the movements of her hands swift and sure. She didn't even glance up from her work as she spoke. "I know. These shallow waters are full of shipwrecks and other debris, and Merriman's ship has that deep smuggling hull full of cargo. We might not fit. But what choice do we have?"

What choice indeed. Aleksy vowed if he ever saw Merriman again, he would punch the traitorous bastard right in the nose. He stared out the window at the ship, now aimed almost directly at their prow. Maybe they ought to ram him. The submarine was iron. She would likely win in a collision. It would serve the pirate right if he lost his ship.

Water began to creep up the window as Nemo guided the ship down. Aleksy murmured a prayer that the lakebed would be deep enough here.

"Ganesha will protect us, too." Nisha nodded toward the tiny statue in the very center of the control panel.

As Aleksy studied the intricately carved elephant god, a light flashed directly into his eye.

"Ow!"

He quickly looked down, blinking to try to clear the spot from his vision. When he raised his head, he shielded his eyes. More flashes assaulted him. They seemed to be coming from the pirate ship.

"What…" he began, before his brain deciphered the pattern. "Oh! Captain! I think Merriman is signaling us. Morse Code. Dot, dot, dot, dash. That's… um… V?"

"Yes."

"Another dot. E. Dash, dot, dot. D." A wave splashed up to the top of the window, blocking his view. At the rate they were sinking, he'd never get the entire message. "I can't see any more."

"It doesn't matter," Nemo bit out. "If he has something to say to me, he can damn well get out of my way and say it to me later. Watch the proximity sensor. I need to know if we're going to hit anything."

Aleksy adjusted his position to get a good view of the panel of lights. "You can do this, Captain. I believe in you."

She looked his direction for no more than a second, but the gentle admiration—maybe even adoration?—in her eyes made his heart skip a beat. They had to get out of this.

They had to. Because he needed to make her look at him that way again.

He snapped his attention back to the lights. If she admired him, he had to be worthy of that. He'd be the best navigator he possibly could.

The lights in the center of the display glowed faintly, a few flickering brighter.

"Ground coming up quickly, Captain. Some places are shallower, but it is uneven."

"Debris. Or rocks." She halted the descent and upped the throttle. "I'm taking us up to speed. Tell me when we're clear to drop lower and prepare for a bumpy ride."

Aleksy's gaze darted back and forth between the display and the window. In the shallow, clear water and bright sunlight, he could see quite well. The low-slung hull of Merriman's ship loomed ahead of them, huge and dark. God, they were so close. The center lights on the panel glowed steadily. No room.

A faint light appeared in the forward portion of the display. Aleksy looked up again, frantically debating his options. Did they stay on course and risk hitting the pirate ship? Or sink lower and possibly run to ground on rocks?

"We should—"

He froze when the bottom compartment of the pirate ship swung open. Long, cylindrical objects tumbled out, falling to the lakebed and rolling away. Relieved of its haul, the steamship rose quickly toward the surface. The cargo doors remained wide open, leaving a narrow path, like a tunnel through the water.

"C-Captain!" Aleksy couldn't form any further words, so he pointed.

Nisha was with him, though. She stared straight ahead,

her brow furrowed in fierce concentration. "I can fit. It'll be tight."

Aleksy gripped the console with sweat-slicked hands. The *Narwhal* hurtled forward, the whir of her steam engines as loud as he'd ever heard. His gaze drifted over the Hindu statuette.

"May God protect us," he whispered. "And may Nisha's Ganesha protect us too."

Aleksy had done all he could. He watched Nisha instead of the pirate ship. She could do this. She *would* do this.

The proximity alarm began to blare. This was it. They were committed. He held his breath, braced for impact.

Noises screamed around him. The alarm. The engines. The rush of the submarine pushing through the water. Yet somehow, the world felt still. Holding its breath along with him. Waiting.

A whoop of triumph cut through the cacophony. Nemo pumped a fist in the air. "Bullseye!"

The pirate ship momentarily blocked out the sun as the submarine darted under it. Moments later, the shadow faded. The alarm fell silent. Finally, Aleksy breathed easy.

"We're free!" Nemo cheered.

He stepped closer and pressed a kiss to her cheek. "You are magnificent."

The appreciative smile that melted his insides appeared again. "Thank you. Can you go to the periscope? Tell me if they're still chasing us. I'm going to keep her at top speed."

Aleksy raced to the engine room and pushed the periscope up, swinging it around until he had a good view of the scene behind them. The pirate ship hadn't altered course, and was now bearing down on Stromberg's vessel.

Aleksy fumbled to switch on the telephonic speaker

in the wall beside him. "Captain, the pirate is maintaining course toward the enemy."

"Thank you," Nemo's crackly voice replied. "I feel vindicated in my belief that he was on our side."

Aleksy scowled. He still didn't like Merriman, but the pirate had dropped his cargo to give them room to escape. And his signals now made sense. He'd been repeating the word "dive."

Aleksy watched the two ships draw closer. "They may collide," he reported.

He flipped a switch on the side of the periscope, and a magnification lens clicked into place. No, the ships weren't going to collide. Stromberg was attempting to turn away. Merriman must have anticipated the tactic, because his ship had also altered course. For a ship of its size, the pirate steamship was shockingly maneuverable. It easily slid into a trajectory that would bring it directly alongside Stromberg's craft.

"What's happening?" Nemo demanded.

"They're…" Aleksy couldn't form words. The two ships came so close together their hulls could have touched. A swarm of at least a dozen men leapt from the pirate ship to the other deck, weapons in hand.

"They're what?" Nemo almost shouted.

"The pirates are storming Stromberg's ship," Aleksy finally replied. "They're attacking. In daylight. I think we're… safe."

He kept watch for a few more minutes, but even with the magnification lens, the two ships rapidly shrank into the distance. He lowered the periscope and spent a moment standing and listening to the whir of the engine, taking stock of himself. His breathing was normal. His pulse had slowed. The twinge of relief he'd felt before was now all-encompassing. They'd escaped. And they were still together.

What did that mean? What did they do now? They couldn't hide or run forever. Even if they eluded or defeated Stromberg, this partnership was still temporary. Eventually, Nemo would depart to continue her explorations and Aleksy would return to trying to make something of himself. He would miss her. He'd miss his time here, doing what he loved.

For today, though, he would appreciate the extra time he'd been given. And he'd help her find a way out of this mess he'd started, if it was the last thing he did.

Chapter 20

Captain's Log, 4 July, 1892
The length of time needed to sail from Milwaukee to Detroit
is giving me great appreciation for train travel.

Nemo stumbled into the galley, her entire body one enormous ache. Did she really need dinner? Maybe tumbling straight into bed would be better. Besides, the food would have gone cold ages ago.

Aleksy scrambled from his seat and rushed over to take her arm. "Come. Sit. Eat." He guided her to her usual place at the table, then pushed three different plates of food toward her. "Eat whatever you like. You need nourishment."

Nemo picked up the fork, knowing he was right. Her body and her brain needed proper nutrition to keep going. And if she intended to push as hard tomorrow as she'd done today, she couldn't neglect that. She ate a bit of salad, then some chicken. It was kind of him to offer her meat, when he didn't eat it himself. Always kind. Always thoughtful.

While she ate, Aleksy heated a pot of water and poured her a large mug of tea.

"Chamomile," he said. He reached across the table and plucked her flask from the pocket just above her hip where it customarily rested. He unscrewed the cap and poured a sizable dose of whiskey into the tea. "It will help you sleep."

"Thank you."

The steaming liquid and strong spirits warmed and relaxed her, soothing away some of the tension built up after the morning's escape and too long at the helm. Perhaps if she drank the whole thing she might be able to rest after all.

"We are safe at the bottom of the lake," Aleksy assured her. Either she was too tired tonight to hide her feelings, or he'd learned to read her too well.

"I think so," she agreed. "But hiding is no longer a viable option. Not if Stromberg has a way to track us. If the pirates have disabled that ship, he will send a new one."

Aleksy propped his elbows on the table and rested his chin in his hands. "But you have an idea."

Nemo swallowed another bite of cold chicken and chased it down with tea. "What makes you say that?"

"You always have ideas. Your brain is very fast. Very busy. You are an engineer. You solve problems."

He said the words as ardently as if he were extolling the beauty of a goddess. Despite her whiskey-laced tisane, her pulse leapt. The longer they remained together, the more fuel he fed to the fire in her heart. How long until she became a volcano, burning for millennia, deep inside?

"Now." He smiled at her. "Tell me your idea."

Nemo sighed. "It's not a good one." There were no good ideas, as far as she could tell. They had a rich, powerful enemy, and that meant danger, no matter what course they took. She slumped over her mug of spiked tea and took a long draught. "I think we need to go on the offensive. We'll return home and go after him however we can. Go to my father, first of all, and explain all we know to the police. Gather additional information as necessary. Somewhere, there must be proof of his wrongdoing."

Aleksy picked up her flask again and took a large gulp

of whiskey. "I wish I had seen or heard something more useful. But the papers were unhelpful. Shipping notices, but not animals. Food and drink. So many boxes of soap. Boring things."

Nemo shot up straight in her seat. "What was that about soap?"

"He bought a lot of it. It wasn't used at the newspaper. Can he be charged for using his own company for personal shipping?"

Soap. Nemo's thoughts whirled, trying to remember the details from her friend Victor's troubles earlier that year.

"Do you remember the name of the soap company, by chance?"

"The name?" Aleksy pursed his lips. "I remember the company symbol. An S. It swirled around like this." He drew a curly S in the air with his finger.

"Simpson Fine Soaps and Lotions?" Nemo suggested.

"Yes!" He grinned. "Yes. It sounded very fancy."

"Baal." Was Stromberg the villain the police had been chasing for years? The one who'd poisoned tonic water and soap and caused trouble first for Hal and then Victor?

Aleksy's smile faded. "What? You have a strange expression on your face."

"I think Stromberg has been making mischief for a long time. Do you remember the incident with the tainted tonic water?"

"I heard of it."

"And then back in January there were more poisonings. Simpson Soaps were among the problem products. It was all over the news. Although not much in the *Mirror*, now that I think on it. That paper was always too busy running articles about drunkards and hoodlums." She banged her fist on the table. "Ugh. It all makes so much sense now!"

"I don't understand."

Nemo blew out a long breath. "When the problem with the tonic water happened, my friend Hal became inadvertently involved. He discovered the product was adulterated. During that time, the papers, particularly the *Mirror*, were painting him and his entire neighborhood as a place full of ruffians and drunken troublemakers. Later, when my friend Victor learned of a new incident of smuggling and poisoning, the *Mirror* started blaming his mechanical man for attacking people. It was all Stromberg. He was using his paper to discredit us. He's the smuggler and the poisoner!"

She fell back against the padded seat back. So much searching. So much stress for her father from the unsolved cases. And now she knew the identity of the man behind it all. If only she had the evidence to back it up.

"We have to stop him," she urged. "We have to expose him before he can execute his next scheme. He probably experiments with his mind-altering products on the animals before using them on people."

"That whoreson," Aleksy growled. "Hurting countless innocents. For what?"

"Control, I think," Nemo replied. "The drugs from his previous schemes were addictive and had the potential to put people into something of a stupor. I suspect he wants the entire world reliant on or subordinate to him."

"That fits with his behavior. He probably wants your submarine to help secretly deliver his poisons."

"And if he realizes how much we know, he may want us both dead."

Aleksy reached across the table and grasped Nisha's hand, his large palm warm and comforting over hers. "I will let no one harm you." His fingertips moved over her skin in spiraling circles. "Nemo nocet Nemo meae."

No one harms my Nemo. Now he was sweet-talking her in Latin. Her volcano heart would be erupting at this rate. But she couldn't regret having him alongside her for a few days more. Pain was inevitable, but she would cherish what she had.

"We will sail to Detroit," Aleksy said in a voice as commanding as she'd ever heard from him. "We will stop this man. And you and your submarine will be safe to explore the world. But tonight, you rest. Finish your dinner. I will clean up."

He whisked away the food she didn't want, stashing it in the icebox, then washing the dishes while she picked at the remains of her salad and chicken. A bit of achiness lingered in her muscles, and the new information about Stromberg was making her head throb. She would go to bed and tomorrow she would be able to think again.

She rose from the table, helped clean and stow the last of the dishes, then headed for her room, Aleksy right behind her.

"Goodnight," he said, as she pushed aside the curtain to step into the cabin.

Nisha spun around. "What are you doing?"

He took a step backward, toward the bunkroom where his things were stored. "You're tired and you need to sleep. I didn't want to presume."

She pointed at her bed. "*We* need sleep. You're sleeping with me in the good bed." She couldn't speak for him, but Nisha knew she would sleep better if he was near. She wanted him as close as possible for as long as possible. Selfish, perhaps, but she'd never claimed to be perfect.

They undressed quickly and crawled beneath the covers. There would be no lovemaking tonight, but somehow that didn't matter. When he curled an arm around her, it filled her with the same sense of peace she felt after sex. She was where she was meant to be: wrapped in his protective embrace. He was her knight in slightly-rumpled clothing. The sun to her moon. Her sleepy brain struggled to remember why she couldn't keep him forever.

Tomorrow. Tomorrow she could sort that out.

For tonight, he was hers.

Chapter 21

Captain's Log, 6 July, 1892
A good explorer must be prepared when things go awry.
Again.

"Location and heading?"

Aleksy's eyes tracked instantly to the correct indicators. After a day and a half of practice, he was finally growing comfortable with the controls. Perhaps Nemo might even be willing to let him pilot the ship unsupervised for a short time.

"Forty-four degrees twenty-seven minutes north, eighty-two degrees eighteen minutes west, heading south-south-east," he replied.

"Excellent. We're making good time. We should reach the southern shores of the lake tonight. We can rest, pick back up in the morning, and be in Detroit by noon."

All throughout the last two days, her manner had been cool and brisk as she manned the helm. Aleksy no longer feared it meant she was holding back from him, however. Come bedtime, she'd be cuddling up with him, full of affection and passion.

He gave her a playful bump with his hip. "Does your timing include my possibly inaccurate steering?"

She returned his flirtatious smile for only a second,

before slipping back into her work mode. "You know you're good enough to maintain a reasonable course now. As long as you don't let your mind wander off and forget to check the gauges."

Aleksy nuzzled her neck. "My mind always wanders when you're nearby. You're very—" He broke off when a flash of light on the echo detector caught his eye. "Obstacle to the left." The light brightened. "We're getting closer to it… no, wait. What?"

The light faded and winked out as quickly as it had appeared. It made no sense. Whatever it was appeared to have moved toward the ship and then away from it. Could it have been a floating chunk of a shipwreck? An error in the equipment?

Another light flashed on and off. Something above them. Then to the right, near the back of the ship.

"Captain, there's something out there."

The proximity alarm let out a single sharp wail, then stopped. Lights flashed across the display in no pattern Aleksy could discern.

Nemo flipped a switch and the outside lights turned on. Ahead of them, the lake was a vast, empty blue, the water slightly hazy.

"Do you see anything?" she asked. "Bits of falling debris? A school of large fish too close to the sensors?"

"Nothing."

She lowered the inside lights. Aleksy scanned the entire bank of windows.

"I don't see—" A shadow of something long and thin snagged in his peripheral vision, and his head snapped around. "Did you see that?"

They both stared at the place where the shadow had appeared. Soon it drifted back into view, clearer now. A long, snaking appendage, attached to an indistinct body. It wriggled toward the submarine, set off the alarm, then retreated.

"It looked like a tentacle," Nisha gasped.

Aleksy's heart jumped. Could it be? Could a species of large cephalopod lurk in the depths of the lakes? He leaned toward the glass, hoping for a better look.

The proximity alarm blared again, and this time it didn't stop. All across the display, lights shone at full brightness. Scraping noises reverberated through the *Narwhal's* steel hull.

"Dammit, it's attacking us!" Nemo jerked the wheel and pulled back on the throttle, turning the ship in a defensive maneuver.

"Don't hurt it! Please don't hurt it!"

"I don't want to hurt it, I want it off my ship." She lunged for the surfacing controls. "Maybe it'll let go if we rise fast enough or high enough."

Aleksy turned for the door. "I'll go to the periscope." Maybe he could get a look at the creature. See what it was doing and if there was a possibility of luring it away. They must have terrified the poor thing. Surely, it had never encountered anything like the submarine in its home.

He had one foot out the door when a sharp *clang* directly overhead made him stop in his tracks.

"That sounded like metal," Nemo blurted. Then she gasped.

Aleksy whirled around. One of the creature's arms dangled across the window. Except this was no cephalopod. Not unless they now grew arms or tentacles out of interlocking iron segments.

"It's a machine!" His words came out in Polish, and he

repeated himself in English as he raced back to Nemo's side. "A machine!"

"Good. That means I don't have to feel bad if I tear its arms off."

She yanked the wheel again. The submarine twisted and turned as much as was possible for such a craft, but all the captain's efforts did nothing to dislodge the mechanical squid device.

An idea sprang fully-formed into Aleksy's mind. "I'm going out in the Minersible."

Nisha lost her grip on the steering wheel. "What? No!"

"I'll be able to get a good look at it," he explained. "The Minersible has tools. I can cut the squid's tether if it's attached to anything. Knock it loose if it's not."

"You've never piloted it by yourself!" she shouted at him, but he was already running for the back of the ship.

"Hold her still!" He called back. "That will be easier for me!"

He thought she might have cursed at him, but between the squid, the engine noise, and the alarms, he couldn't make out the words. He darted into the aft compartment, sealed the door, and climbed into the Minersible.

Oh, God, what am I doing?

There was that impulsive streak, sending him hurtling into danger. Maybe Nisha was right to curse him.

He let his fingers run over the various switches and dials, thinking back to the way her hands had moved when she'd been at his side. He missed the feel of her body touching his in the small space. Today, she had a different job to do. It was Aleksy's turn to show what he'd learned from her. He reached for the knob that would release the vehicle and open the exit ramp.

Water crept up around him, as the metal squid continued to scratch and bang on the outside of the ship.

Hurry up, hurry up.

If the squid did serious damage, the *Narwhal* could flood or become stranded hundreds of feet beneath the surface.

Aleksy's hands clenched on the handlebars. "Never," he vowed. He'd promised he wouldn't let anyone hurt Nisha, and he was going to keep that promise or die trying.

The moment the ramp fell open, he pedaled the Minersible into action. As he sailed out into the open water, he tested the controls for the claw arm and the slicer. Both he could use one-handed, while maintaining a grip on the handlebars. Whoever was controlling that squid was going to wish he'd stayed away.

The Minersible's lights weren't as powerful as those on the *Narwhal*, but they cast a wide enough arc for Aleksy to survey the round body of the squid machine and the dangling, twitching tentacles.

Whatever the tentacles were meant for, it wasn't attack. They had no discernible claws for grabbing, and the ends were blunt rather than pointed. The pilot of the machine—assuming it had one—was attempting to maneuver the squid along the top of the ship.

Aleksy drew closer. The place where a real squid's beak would have been was taken up by an oval-shaped hatch, ringed with rubber and large enough to fit snugly around the entrance to the *Narwhal*. The squid twisted and banged its arms, trying to align the two hatches.

"You do not get to invade her ship, you son of a whore," Aleksy snarled.

He aimed the Minersible directly at the squid. If the vehicle had windows, they weren't on this side. The enemy would never see him coming.

Aleksy clamped the Minersible's claw arm onto one of the squid's limbs. A flick of a switch, and he had the saw arm spinning. It screeched in victory, tearing into the enemy appendage. The iron tentacle fell away, plunging into the dark depths below.

Aleksy steered the Minersible to the next arm and repeated the procedure. Two down. Then three. The squid began to thrash. He aimed for a spinning propeller to prevent any chance of escape.

The two whirling blades came together with a squealing, tearing racket that made Aleksy wince, even through the water and the thick glass surrounding him. The Minersible jolted and the saw arm stalled out. But so did the enemy.

Aleksy seized one of the remaining arms with his claw, then positioned the damaged saw arm a few inches above the *Narwhal's* hull.

Dot, dot, dot, he tapped out with the arm. *Dot, dot, dash. Dot, dash, dot.*

Methodically, he banged out the word, hoping Nemo would hear and understand him.

S-U-R-F-A-C-E. S-U-R-F-A-C-E.

The ship began to rise. Aleksy checked the grip of the claw arm. Still firm. The body of the squid remained motionless, though the tentacles continued to flop.

The ride to the surface dragged on. Aleksy's legs began to cramp. He didn't dare release the steering mechanisms for either the Minersible or the claw arm. This enemy wasn't getting away from him.

After what felt like hours, the ship broke the surface. She bounced for a moment, then settled into a steady float.

Aleksy relaxed his grip on the controls and opened the Minersible's hatch. He scrambled out of the small boat, picked his way over the slippery surface of the submarine, and hammered on the squid's hatch with a fist.

"Show yourself, you bastard!"

He pounded and pounded, again and again until the hatch shifted beneath his hand. He slipped a bit as he sprang back, but managed to retain his footing and properly brace himself to meet the enemy as the hatch opened.

A bleary-eyed man stumbled out, a pistol clutched in his trembling hand.

"Did you mean to harm the captain?" Aleksy demanded, as if he had the upper hand.

The man waved the pistol in a haphazard fashion. "I was going to storm the ship. Subdue her. Take over."

Aleksy curled his fingers into a fist and plowed it into the man's jaw. The villain dropped like a stone, the pistol clattering to the deck and sliding off into the water.

"No one hurts her," Aleksy spat at the unconscious man. "No. One." He grabbed the man's legs and dragged him toward the Minersible.

Chapter 22

Captain's Log, 6 July, 1892
In all the many designs I made while planning this ship, I
never thought to include a brig.

Nemo waved the smelling salts beneath the enemy's nose. He twitched, then groaned.

"Good," she declared. "You're awake."

The minion made a garbled noise. He wiggled, then seemed to realize his hands and feet had been bound. They'd shoved him into Nemo's usual seat at the table, since the *Narwhal* wasn't equipped with any better place to interrogate a prisoner.

The man slumped, accepting his defeat. Dark circles ringed his eyes, and his skin had a sallow cast. He looked like he hadn't slept in days.

Nemo folded her arms across her chest and glared down at him. "You're going to tell us who you are, who you're working for, and why you attacked us with that squid apparatus."

He sniffed. "I'm not telling you anything."

"Oh, I think you will." Aleksy slid into the seat across from the man, his favorite kitchen knife in his hand. A feral smile played across his lips. Silently, he skimmed a finger across the edge of the blade to test the sharpness.

The minion gulped.

Aleksy leaned forward, still playing with the knife, and snarled a long string of Polish words, none of which Nemo recognized.

"Fine, fine!" The man attempted to press himself as flat against the wall as possible. "I'll talk. Don't let him cut me!"

"You work for Talon Stromberg," Nisha said, leaving no doubt in her tone. "Was that his squid boat?"

"She's mine!" the minion cried. "I built her! I perfected her sonar appendages!"

"What's sonar?"

He smirked. "Sound navigation and ranging. Using sound waves to determine the locations and distances of objects. It's a highly sophisticated—"

"Like my echo-detector," Nemo interrupted. "That explains how they've been tracking us. I assume you were responsible for those strange noises and knocks we heard in the past, then. Where are the others? Where's the steamship?"

"Captured by pirates," the man snorted. "I snapped the tether and came after you myself."

"To capture us for Stromberg?"

"To capture you for myself! Stromberg underestimated you. Didn't think you'd be making deals with pirates. My octo-pod needs to go up for air. She can't stay under like this ship can. I wanted to learn your secrets. Where is the octo-pod? What have you done with her?"

"At the bottom of the lake," Aleksy replied cheerily. "I pushed it off. It sank very quickly."

The minion moaned as if in physical pain. His entire body drooped, as whatever spirit he still had drained out of him.

"What does Stromberg want?" Nemo demanded. "Does he want to kill us? Capture us? Poison us with Sobridyne?"

The man's eyes widened for a split second. Ah. So he hadn't expected them to know that detail.

"That's his goal, isn't it? To sneak addictive substances into things in order to control people?" she pressed.

The man shrugged. Aleksy tapped the knife on the table.

"I don't know!" the minion pleaded. "I've heard nothing like that."

Nemo didn't believe him, but she nodded for him to continue.

"Stromberg is a genius," he said dully, as if repeating something he'd memorized. "He is recruiting others of great intelligence, great skill, or great power to assist him in bettering the world. All who are weak or need guidance will turn to us for leadership. It is the natural order of things."

Nisha rolled her eyes. "Of course he's a Social Darwinist."

"Yes!" A spark of hope entered the minion's expression. "You have thwarted and eluded him. You should join us!"

"Ha!" Aleksy scoffed.

The minion persisted. "Let me free and we will sail the submarine together to Stromberg. He's angry with you for harboring a criminal, but if we take this knife-wielding fiend to him, he'll forgive you. It will lead to greatness. Your inventions will be used around the world. Every household from California to the Atlantic coast will know your name. You will be showered with praise and adoration. Give him up and join us and you will have everything you've ever desired!"

Oh, yes. Betraying the love of her life to an enemy and

letting someone else control her future was exactly what she'd always desired. How could she have been so foolish?

She gestured for Aleksy to follow her and walked toward the sleeping quarters, pausing where she could still see Stomberg's man, but far enough to whisper without being heard.

Aleksy hurried to her side and leaned toward her ear. "He doesn't know you at all. You don't love fame and fortune. You love science."

"I don't know if he's even thinking clearly. He looks ready to keel over. And he's terrified of you."

"Good." Aleksy tested the knife's edge once again.

"I don't know what to do with him. We have no place to put him. We can't take him to Detroit. We may have to stop and release him."

"Tak." Aleksy raised his voice to a normal volume and asked, "Do you think he can swim?"

Nemo shook her head. "I think you can stop tormenting him now," she murmured.

Aleksy looked her straight in the eye, his expression hard. "He meant to harm you."

Nemo nocet Nemo meae. Of course his protective instincts were aroused. She wouldn't have been terribly surprised to discover he belonged to a secret society of scholar-warriors.

She patted his chest. "Thank you. You've protected me valiantly. Oh, and what was that you growled at him in Polish? Did you threaten to cut off his balls?"

Aleksy grinned. "I said, 'I must sharpen this knife before I cook dinner.'"

A half-snorted laugh burst out of her. "You are terrible. Let's surface and find a bit of empty coastline where we can drop him. It will delay our arrival in Detroit, but I think it's the only way."

Another delay. A few extra hours with her gallant knight. She stepped away from him and walked toward the control room, her hands suddenly shaky. They had one more night together. She was going to make it a night to remember.

Chapter 23

Captain's Log, 6 July, 1892
I don't want him to leave.

Conveniently, their captive did know how to swim. Nemo found an unoccupied stretch of Canadian coastline, and Aleksy happily threw the man into the lake to dog paddle his way to shore.

Now, hours later, the satisfaction of thwarting an enemy still thrummed in his veins. Another of Nisha's mother's dishes had left his belly pleasantly full. Now he was contemplating which Polish foods to share first when they reached Detroit tomorrow. All, in all, an excellent evening.

And one that was about to get even better.

Nisha had been casting amorous glances in his direction since dinner. Every twitch of her eyebrows and quirk of her mouth had sent bolts of desire arcing through him. The time had come to give the lady exactly what she wanted. He would start with her hands, pressing his lips to her knuckles, then up her arms, to her throat, her lips, then down her torso. Or perhaps he'd begin at her feet and make his way up her shapely legs. Both, probably. He intended to kiss her all over.

He shucked his clothing, piled it neatly on his bunk, then strode across the hall, no longer the slightest bit concerned about strolling into her room naked. She didn't even pull the curtain closed anymore.

Her coveralls, boots, and stockings were gone, leaving her in a corset and combinations. Aleksy leaned against the door jamb, content to let her take her time exposing all her gorgeous skin to his view.

"I have arrived at the right time." When her head turned, he gave her an appreciative grin and a wink.

Nisha's hot gaze caressed him head to toe. His cock, already half hard, stiffened to full attention.

"Isn't it fascinating," she remarked, opening the top clasp of her corset, "the various stimuli that can cause arousal?" Her fingers slid down the silky fabric to the next metal clip.

Pop.

Aleksy's mouth watered.

"Oh, yes," he replied. "States of undress. Partial undress, to hint at what is underneath. And many non-visual things. The sound of a lover's voice. The brush of a hand."

"The scent of freshly washed skin." Nisha inhaled deeply. "The taste of eager lips."

Alesky forced himself to remain lounging in the doorway. Her corset was half unfastened now, and he was sorely tempted to yank it off of her.

"I'm ready to taste, now," he teased. "In many different locations. It is good to gather as much data as possible."

Nisha dropped the corset and reached for the buttons on her combinations. The garment was opaque, sadly, but it clung to her breasts in a way that revealed the shape of her taut nipples. Aleksy was definitely going to suck those.

"I can tell you're hungry." She laughed. "You keep licking your lips."

"You make me hungry. I adore the taste of you. I love

the feel of your skin against mine. I want to bask in your flowery scent."

"Jasmine. My mother imports the perfume from a traditional shop in Calcutta."

"It's beautiful. I love how you enjoy things called feminine, like flowers and diamonds. And things called masculine, like trousers and engineering. You do not force yourself to be what people say. You are just you, and that is beautiful."

"I think you're beautiful too." She shimmied out of the combinations, leaving herself wearing nothing but a smile so joyful, his knees went suddenly weak.

God, this woman. She was strong, passionate, kind, funny, scholarly, and creative. Everything he would want in a lover. Everything he would want in a partner.

His heart skipped a beat.

I love her. I love her and I never want to let her go.

But was he worthy of her? How could he support a wife when he had no money? And what about the looming obstacle of Stromberg and his crew? So many things remained to be sorted out, if Aleksy were to have any hope. Still, he wanted to try. He wanted to see if they could invent a future where they could be together.

He straightened up, took one step into the room, and swept her into his arms. "My siren," he murmured. "You lured me out to sea, and now I am lost."

Their lips came together in a slow, tender kiss he could have reveled in for days. He tasted the full curve of each soft lip, savoring every subtle movement. When her hands wandered down his back, he did the same to her.

Little by little, the kiss deepened. Their hands explored further, caressing buttocks and torsos. Fingers rubbed and rolled over nipples.

"The bed," Nisha gasped. "Now."

They tumbled together, their kisses becoming ravenous, possessive. Aleksy couldn't tell and didn't care whether he was claiming her or the other way around.

Magnificent. Perfect. He would never get enough of her. But he could give himself temporary satisfaction. It was time to kiss her all over, as he'd planned. The only question remaining was where to start. Neck? Hands? Feet? Breasts?

Before he could decide, Nisha rolled on top of him, pushing him onto his back. Her thighs clamped around his, and she flattened both hands on his chest to brace herself.

Aleksy smiled up at her. Very well. If she wanted to go first, she could. When she finished, he would ensure that he reciprocated with the utmost thoroughness.

She adjusted her position, letting out a murmur of pleasure when she slid along the length of his cock.

Aleksy sucked in a sudden breath. Good Lord, that felt good. Slick and warm. Inviting. They hadn't tried this before, but he was entirely in favor of letting her rub against him until she brought them both to completion.

He reached up to fondle her breasts as she rocked, flicking and lightly pinching her nipples in the way he now knew she liked best. Her lusty sighs and the gyration of her hips made his head swim. Incredible, that's what she was. Everything about her was incredible. Every moment he shared with her increased his certainty that he needed a lifetime of her.

"Aleksy," she moaned, moving faster, pressing herself harder against his cock. "I want you. Please."

He lowered his hands to grasp her hips, undulating in time to her movements.

"Please," Nisha repeated. "I want you inside me."

Aleksy froze. He wanted that too. Wanted it with every fiber of his being. But she'd forbidden it from the start.

"What of the rules?"

She twitched atop him, her body insisting on more. "Damn the rules. I want this. I need you."

"Anything you desire." How could he refuse her, when he adored her so? He wanted nothing more than to give her every pleasure, every joy.

She rose up, and together they aligned their bodies until she could sink down atop him, taking his cock fully inside her. His groan of bliss mingled with hers, filling the small chamber. Their chamber. Their bed.

"Kocham Cię," he gasped.

And then he could say no more. His fingers tightened on her hips and he thrust upward to meet her every downward stroke. Pure ecstasy. Every muscle in his body clenched tight as he strained to maintain control. He had to last. She had to come first.

"Yes." The single pleading syllable escaped her throat when he reached between them and stroked a finger over her clitoris. "Y-yes." Her head fell back, her hair tumbling in wild curls around her shoulders. "A-Aleksy!"

Nisha trembled and shook, her mouth open, eyes closed. Her cry was one of unsurpassable pleasure. Glorious. And all for him.

Aleksy hardly had time to register the tingle at the bottom of his spine through the delirium of his own gratification. He spasmed and jerked, barely pulling free of her body before spending everything he had.

Nisha rolled off him and curled up at his side, slinging an arm across his chest and nuzzling his neck. "Thank you," she sighed, before letting out a lengthy yawn.

Aleksy brushed a lock of her hair aside and pressed a

kiss to her temple. She'd been working so hard the last few days. With luck, she would fall into a deep, relaxing slumber.

"Kocham Cię," he murmured. *I love you.* He stopped short of repeating the words in English. When he said that to her, he wanted her fully awake and aware.

"Thank you," she said again, her voice slow and sleepy.

"Thank *you*, najdroższa. You were perfect."

"Mmm." She gave another small yawn and her eyes drifted closed. "I… needed that. Needed… you. Before… end."

Aleksy flinched. Nisha lay still, her breathing soft and steady, fast asleep.

End? What did she mean by that? Could she…

He pressed a palm to his face. What had he been thinking? This was their last night on the submarine. Their last night sharing a bed. Tomorrow, they would be… somewhere. Perhaps at home, perhaps in hiding. But they would no longer be together.

A cold fist clamped around his heart. They might never be together again. How tragic, for this perfect night to be the last. The last touch. The last kiss.

He kissed her cheek, letting his lips linger against her skin. He breathed in her jasmine perfume and stroked her lovely hair.

Finally, he turned away.

She shifted in her sleep, snuggling up against his back. Aleksy held himself perfectly still as silent tears streamed down his cheeks.

Chapter 24

Captain's Log, 7 July, 1892
Arrival in Detroit. It feels wrong, leaving my Narwhal *alone*
at the marina. I'll be tipping one of the dockhands extra to
take particular care of her.

The omnibus rounded the corner onto a brightly-lit street lined with mansions. Aleksy gaped as they flew by house after house, all stately brick and hand-worked stone. Wrought iron fences protected lawns as neat as a park, and electric lights twinkled from nearly every window. The towering arc lights sent sharp beams of light crisscrossing the road.

Nisha nudged him when the bus began to slow. "This is our stop."

He turned his slack-jawed expression on her. This was her neighborhood? This street of millionaires? How much money did a chief of police earn? Or did she come from old money? God, there were so many things he didn't know about her.

She led him off the bus and past several houses, to a handsome brick structure, three stories tall and as wide as Aleksy's whole apartment building. He trudged up the front steps, running his fingers over the intricately carved scrollwork handrail.

Nisha rapped on the door, and it opened within seconds.

A tall man with graying blond hair and pale, freckled cheeks waved them in.

"Miss Majhi, how lovely to have you back home."

"Thank you, Jasper. Is my father at home? I have urgent business with him."

"He is in his study taking a telephone call," Jasper answered. "I will let him know you have arrived. In the meantime, your mother and grandmother are in the east parlor."

"Thank you."

"My pleasure, miss." The butler bowed and walked off down the hall.

Aleksy's stomach churned. Dear God, she had servants. Her house was like a palace. She was so far above him, he may as well have been an ant, skittering across the ground, waiting to be stepped on. What did he do? How did he act? He was a janitor, for Christ's sake!

"East parlor?" The words almost squeaked out of him. "How many parlors do you have?"

"East and west." Captain Nemo was as cool as ever. To her, this was normal life. "The west parlor is small and we only use it for visitors. The east parlor is for family. Follow me, it's just through this door."

What could he do but comply? He trailed after her, suddenly all too conscious of his off-the-rack suit and old shoes.

The east parlor was an elegant melding of European and Indian aesthetics. Gorgeous jewel-toned fabrics paired with dark wood. Delicate organic patterns accented the simple lines of Arts-and-Crafts furniture.

Two women sat in opposite corners, intent on their work. The woman to Aleksy's right had to be Nemo's mother. Except for slight differences around the eyes and nose, she could have been an older version of Nisha. Her glossy hair was piled atop her head, and an emerald-green sari shrouded her body. In her hands, she held a needle and thread, stitching shimmering gold embroidery onto the most beautiful red fabric he had ever seen.

Her face lit up when she spied her daughter. "Nisha, shona, you are home! And you've brought a young man with you. How wonderful!" She held up the garment she was working on. "Ami matro tomar biyer sharir upor kaj korchilam." She turned to Aleksy. "This is to be her wedding dress."

Nisha went rigid. Aleksy cringed. He was one hundred percent certain his mother would have made a similar comment had they gone to his home instead. Maybe they should have gone their separate ways.

"We have business with Father," Nisha said, a distinct edge to her voice. Aleksy could sympathize. Reining in one's emotions was always more difficult with those you were close to.

"You've always been an efficient sort of girl," said the other woman. She was older, her hair gone gray and her face lined from years of smiling. She wore an American-style dress and sat in a rocking chair, sketching in a notebook. "Of course you would accomplish multiple tasks at once. Now, introduce us to your young man, little Nemo."

Nisha sighed, then composed herself. "Dadi, Mother, may I introduce Mr. Aleksy Szekalski, a brilliant biologist. Aleksy, this is my Dadi—my father's mother—and my mother. Both go by Mrs. Majhi."

"Mrs. Majhi and Mrs. Majhi. A pleasure to meet you." Aleksy nodded first to Nisha's grandmother, then to her mother, trying to adopt his own version of captain's calm, though his cheeks were burning.

Nisha had called him brilliant. And introduced him as a biologist, as if it were his legitimate profession. Also, she'd called him by his first name in a formal introduction. Would her family take that as confirmation of their assumptions?

Clearly she hadn't brought him here for such a purpose, but she also hadn't denied anything. Perhaps he had some small hope of winning her. He didn't belong in her luxurious world, but his longing for her hadn't ebbed in the slightest. Two warring urges filled him. The first: to find her father and beg for her hand. The second: to flee.

"Nisha, come see your sari." Her mother waved a hand to beckon her. "I want to see if it suits you."

It would absolutely suit her. With the red against her warm skin and the gold echoing the lighter flecks in her dark eyes, she would shine like the sun. Aleksy would surrender all his earthly possessions to stand beside her when she wore that silk.

Nisha obediently walked to her mother's side, though her jaw clenched and her posture remained stiff. Aleksy followed. He had no real purpose here, but he could give her support.

"What do you think, dear?" Mrs. Majhi spread out the fabric to display the embroidery. She placed the piece of paper she was working from beside it. "Have I gotten it right?"

Aleksy frowned down at the lines of gold thread and the matching diagram. Was that a schematic drawing?

Nemo gasped. Aleksy's gaze flew to her face. She had a hand over her mouth. Tears welled in her eyes.

"That's my submarine," she choked.

"Of course it is, darling," her mother replied. "I want you to be you on your special day."

Nisha swiped at her eyes. Her gaze flicked toward

Aleksy, and for an instant the world ceased moving around them.

"I love it," she whispered.

I love you. The words danced on the tip of his tongue. He needed to say them. He needed to pour out his feelings to her, even if it marked the end of everything. At least he would know he'd tried.

Her grandmother's voice broke the spell. "Our Nisha comes from a long line of mechanical geniuses. I was not surprised when she crafted something to rival the work of the older generations." She turned her notebook around to display what looked like an engineer's sketch of a steam car. "Come, my Nemo. Tell me how you like my newest ideas."

"Your grandmother designs steam cars?" he blurted.

"I invented the steam car, boy!" The old woman grinned. "It's why I came to this country. Mr. Welmar was searching for a self-propelled vehicle to produce in his factory. My design won, so I brought the family to Detroit to help him with the manufacturing. All those Welmar auto cabs rolling down the street? My design. He hasn't bought my latest yet. He's lagging behind. If you need a properly fast car, there's a prototype out back."

"Thank you. That sounds interesting." A true smile spread across his face for the first time since he'd left the submarine.

Of course her grandmother was an engineer. Of course her mother embroidered submarines onto a wedding dress. Nisha had always shown genuine affection when speaking of her family. These were the people who loved her and had supported her as she'd grown into the woman she was today.

A surge of rightness filled him. So what if his social standing was barely above that of a sewer rat. This was a family he could belong to. A family who would join him in his goal of giving Nisha a life of love and happiness. Somehow, some way, he would make it happen. He would find that future, even if it meant diving to the very bottom of the ocean.

"Nisha," a man's low voice spoke from behind them. "You've brought a friend with you. I gather you have news for us?"

Aleksy turned around. "Mr. Mahji." He nodded to the older man. "Aleksy Szekalski. It's a pleasure to meet you."

And if I can convince Nisha to have me, I'd like to ask for her hand in marriage.

Chapter 25

Captain's Log, 7 July, 1892
Here's hoping we have enough information for the police to do something about Stromberg.

"Father," Nemo interjected before anyone could make any further insinuations about Aleksy's presence. "We have important information regarding the man responsible for the rash of strange, addictive substances these past two years."

His dark eyebrows shot upward. "That case again? Nisha, how is it your friends are always tangled in these things?"

My friends are intelligent, observant, and unendingly curious. They notice unusual things and then have to investigate.

She was the same. So was Aleksy. He would fit into their group as seamlessly as Callie and Mary had done.

Nisha nearly turned to glance back at her submarine wedding sari.

Don't. Not now.

That future couldn't be contemplated. Not when Aleksy had been off the submarine for no more than an hour. He deserved time and space to make his own choices, whether they included her or not.

Nisha's father waved a hand at the door. "Why don't we go to my study and discuss this?"

They trekked down the hall, Aleksy trailing behind. He had to be as embarrassed as she was about her family's matchmaking. Though their assumptions weren't wholly unreasonable. She'd never brought a man into the house before, and she'd been friends with Victor and Hal for many years.

When they reached the study, Nisha's father settled into his plush chair behind his desk. He pushed the telephone to one side to give himself a clear view and set blank paper and pen in the center of the desk.

Nisha and Aleksy took the two guest chairs by the wall and arranged themselves opposite her father. Aleksy placed his chair a respectable distance from hers, but at such an angle that their feet could touch if they both stretched their legs out.

It also meant they could comfortably watch one another during the conversation. His blue-gray eyes made a swift perusal of her as she sat.

Nemo's pulse beat faster. The connection between them hadn't faded in the presence of others. Would it diminish with time? Would they begin to shift back to their lives from before they met?

Her father picked up his pen, preventing her from dwelling on her romantic issues. "Tell me what you've learned."

"The villain's name is Talon Stromberg, the owner of the *Detroit Mirror*," she answered.

His eyebrows arched. "That's quite the accusation."

"Yes." Nisha nodded at Aleksy. "Why don't you begin by telling him what you discovered at work."

Aleksy took his time relaying his discovery of the smuggled animals, pausing here and there to think. As far as Nemo could tell, he didn't miss a single detail. Her father made notes as Aleksy related everything: the axolotl, the papers, the suspicious deliveries from Simpson Soaps.

When he finally finished, she took over, wracking her brain for every sighting and encounter with Stromberg's men. Her father's jaw clenched when she reached their flight from Lake Michigan and the squid machine attack, but he didn't interrupt.

"We dropped the man off in Canada, then sailed here to tell you everything," Nisha finished. *After a night of unrestrained passion that I will never forget as long as I live.*

She would do it all again. The hiding, the running, the fear. Every bit of it would be worth more nights in Aleksy's arms.

Her father's pen stopped scratching. "My goodness, Nisha." He squeezed his eyes closed and pressed a hand to his face for several seconds. "I am relieved you were not hurt. I will convey this information to the investigative team."

"But you can't arrest Stromberg." She didn't even bother to make it a question. Growing up with the chief of police, she knew well how the force operated.

"Everything you've told me points to him as our man. But none of it is firm proof. If we want to arrest him or search his home and office, we need a witness or a piece of clear evidence."

"And if we can bring you that?"

"We would arrest him, naturally." Her father shook his head. "But Nisha, do not go sneaking about looking for it. I do not want you in danger or committing crimes of your own."

"We will not commit crimes, Chief Majhi," Aleksy

said in a firm and surprisingly sincere voice. "You have my word." He wore a hint of a smile.

Nisha gave him a questioning frown, but he only continued to smile.

"We should depart now," he declared. He rose from his seat and offered Nisha a hand up.

She placed her hand in his, letting him help her to her feet. Knowing the touch would spark a rush of desire didn't make it any less powerful. Her whole body vibrated. Her arms tensed against the urge to fling her arms around him. Their eyes met, freezing her where she stood.

"Is there anything else you two wish to tell me while you're here?" her father asked.

Nemo tore her gaze away from Aleksy, releasing his hand a moment later. "No. If we learn anything else, we will return or telephone."

Her father looked back and forth between her and Aleksy, then sighed. "Please be careful, Daughter."

"I promise. I love you, Father." She walked around the desk and gave him a peck on the cheek. "We'll be back as soon as we're able."

He hooked an arm around her waist and hugged her tight. "You may be full grown, but you will always be my little adventurer." His gaze turned to Aleksy. "Protect her."

"With my life," Aleksy vowed.

Nisha pulled abruptly from her father's embrace. She strode toward the door, not daring to look at either man, lest it cause the tears gathering in her eyes to overflow. She was independent, competent, fully able to take care of herself. But that didn't mean she didn't need anyone. The support and love of her family and friends helped her be her best self, and she adored them, each and every one.

By the time she stepped out the front door, she'd

recovered her composure. Tears and sentimentality could come later. Tonight she had work to complete. She bounded down the stairs and turned right onto the sidewalk. Captain Nemo was calling an emergency meeting of the Mad Scientists Society.

"Nisha?"

She paused.

Aleksy touched her arm. "Where are you going?"

"To my friend Victor's house. My friends have tangled with Stromberg in the past. They may be able to help us find the proof we need."

"Ah. I think we should search his office. He is an organized man. He will have records."

Was that the idea that had made him smile in the study? Nisha liked the straightforwardness of it, but wasn't certain that outweighed the risks.

"You heard my father. No crime. We can't break in."

Aleksy's grin shone as bright as the streetlight above him. He reached deep inside his coat and withdrew a ring with half-a-dozen keys dangling from it.

"We will not break in. I have keys and no one has said my employment is ended. I am the janitor." He winked. "There is much cleaning to do."

Chapter 26

The massive grandfather clock in the lavish Franklin sitting room tolled midnight. Nemo's friends sat quietly, pondering everything she'd told them. On the red velvet sofa, Callie unwound herself from Hal's embrace to check on the baby she carried nestled in a sling. A sleek stone hearth separated them from Victor and Mary, who occupied the gold sofa. They didn't cuddle, but their arms and legs touched, and their gazes met frequently.

Nemo shifted in the armchair she'd selected. Jealousy gnawed at her. The one thing she truly wanted right now was to be curled up with Aleksy. On a sofa, a bed, the floor. Anywhere but these too-far-apart chairs, watching her friends exchange intimate looks and touches.

The clock fell silent.

Victor spoke first. "I think you've cracked our case, Nemo. I can't think of anything else I know that might constitute proof, unfortunately." He glanced at his wife. "How about you?"

"Nothing comes to mind," Mary replied. "I believe we told you all we knew when he was after us."

"Exactly," Hal added. "We shared everything with the police and now you've done the same."

Callie yanked her dress down, not caring in the slightest that everyone could see her naked breast, and set the baby to nursing. "You must have a plan, though. What is it?"

Nisha motioned for Aleksy to take over.

Aleksy jingled his keys and held them aloft for everyone to see. Studiously avoiding looking at Callie, he explained his idea. "In two hours, all printing will be over and the newspaper building will close. The morning shift begins after dawn. While the building is quiet, I will go to my job, cleaning and gathering trash. Stromberg's office must be very dirty and will need my attention."

Victor chuckled. "And the rest of us come along for an early morning tour?"

"Like that, yes. It may be partly illegal." Aleksy shrugged.

"We're going anyway," Hal insisted. "The more of us there are, the faster we can search for evidence."

Nemo rose from her chair. "Agreed. We all go. We should rest now. Sleep if you can. At three o'clock we'll depart. That will be safely between working hours."

"I'll wake everyone when Sienna needs to nurse again," Callie offered. "The timing should be almost perfect."

"Can you rest well enough here?" Mary asked. "The castle has guest rooms if necessary."

"I'll be fine here," Callie replied. "I can use this sofa and Hal can take the other. You can give the guest rooms to Nisha and Mr. Szekalski."

Aleksy shook his head fervently. "No, no. I don't need a room. I can sleep in a chair."

Victor pushed to his feet. "This house has five different sitting rooms. Come with me. I'll show you to another sofa."

He led Aleksy and Nisha further into the mansion, to a sitting room much like the other, but decorated in blues and greens.

"The chaise is the more comfortable of the two," Victor said. "You two can wrestle for it." He gave Nemo a wink as he headed for the door.

She frowned at him.

Aleksy, who hadn't noticed the interaction, walked to the chaise to examine it.

Victor altered his course to pause at Nemo's side. "Don't tell me you don't want to," he whispered.

Nisha sniffed.

"All night he's been giving you looks that could melt steel," her friend murmured. "And some people might not notice you squirming in response, but I've known you for too long. You want him."

She couldn't deny it. The volcano inside her was primed for an explosion. Her gaze drifted to Aleksy just in time to see him sprawl on the chaise and tuck his hands behind his head.

"This is excellent," he declared. "I will fight you for it."

Here comes the bride, Victor hummed. He gave Nemo another wink and departed.

Nemo flung herself onto the less-comfortable couch and closed her eyes. In her head, the song played on.

* * *

Every jingle of the keys sent a frisson of fear down Nemo's spine. Her father would be furious. If they were caught in an illegal act, the police would likely reject any evidence they'd found. And if Stromberg's guards spied them...

"Quickly," Aleksy whispered. He waved everyone inside, then closed and locked the door behind them.

The group huddled in the darkness, listening for any sign they may have been discovered. Nemo fingered her watch, the gentle *tick, tick* vibrating through her hand.

Twenty-six seconds later, Aleksy spoke in a soft voice. "The guards would be here if they had seen us. Follow me."

With the lights on, Nisha knew the way to Stromberg's office. In the dark, she could hardly get her bearings, even as her eyes began to adjust. Aleksy, though, knew the building as if he'd been born there. He navigated all six adults and one baby safely past printing presses, down corridors, and up six flights of stairs, before pausing in front of a door.

"This is a janitorial closet," he said, sliding a key into the lock. He swung the door open, reached in, and turned on a small lantern. "This is the light I use if I work at night. My employer—" He added an extra snarl to the word. "Doesn't like wasteful use of electricity."

Aleksy pulled out a trash bin on wheels and a battered rag. Leaving the closet open, he wheeled the bin to the next door over and unlocked it. The whole group squeezed into Stromberg's office, circling the sleek mahogany desk.

The room needed no cleaning. The floor was spotless, the two large shelves tidy, and not a speck of dust to be seen. Stomberg's chair was pushed beneath the desk, and the guest chairs sat in the corners on either side of the door.

To the right, a large portrait of Stromberg himself covered a portion of the wall. Even in the idealized painting, he was a man of average appearance: sallow of complexion, with dull gray-brown hair and an unremarkable stature. His expression, however, was one of supreme superiority. He stood with one hand propped on his hip, while a fluffy white cat nestled in the crook of his other arm. From the placement of the painting, he appeared to smirk down at the observer from every angle.

What a jackass.

"Filthy place," Victor remarked. "We'd better check every nook and cranny so you can clean it."

They leapt into action, peeking in drawers, rifling through papers, looking on, under, and behind everything. Stromberg kept his office meticulously organized. Current papers were arranged on the desk. Older documents were stored in binders on shelves. Nemo flipped through book after book, finding nothing of use. With every minute that passed, her muscles tightened more.

We'll be caught. We'll be caught and for nothing.

"There's nothing here." Callie put her hands on her hips. "I'm a librarian. I understand this man's organization. The evidence will all be together and neatly arranged. It must be hidden."

Hal put a hand on his wife's shoulder. "Then we look for a hiding place. A secret drawer or a hidden safe."

Aleksy lifted the lantern and swung it in a slow circle. When the light fell on Stromberg's portrait, he paused.

"Do you think there's a safe behind it?" Mary wondered. She walked to the painting and tugged on the frame. It didn't move.

"No. A room." Aleksy came around the desk to Mary's side. He touched the wall eight or ten inches from the portrait. "The janitorial closet is only this deep. What is behind it?"

He set the lantern on the desk, aimed it at the wall, and began to run his hands up and down the smooth paneling. Victor did the same on the opposite side of the portrait.

"I don't see any seams where a door could be," Victor sighed. He dropped to the floor. "If there's a door, there must be a crack somewhere along the floor."

Nemo surveyed the wall, mulling over what she knew of Stromberg. He certainly had the ego to hide important things behind a portrait of himself, but he wouldn't be obvious about it.

Her gaze drifted down to the pair of potted plants below the painting. Tucked between them was a wooden step stool, meant for retrieving books from the top shelves. Or, maybe, stepping into a secret room.

Nisha squeezed past her friends, pulled the stool away from the wall, and climbed to the top step. From this vantage point, the painted Stromberg was no longer smirking at her. Instead he looked slightly down and to the right.

Her engineer's brain automatically calculated the angles. No. Stromberg was about two inches taller than her. She rose up on her toes and adjusted the numbers. There. The eyes of his likeness tracked exactly to a point in the center of the ornate gilded frame. Nemo placed her finger in the right place and pushed.

The sudden *clunk* was so loud she wobbled and would have fallen if not for Aleksy's hand pressing into her back and steadying her.

"I have you."

Ahead of them, the portrait swung inward. An electric light clicked on, revealing a small chamber beyond.

Aleksy rubbed a tiny circle against her back. "I have you, brilliant Nisha."

His hand withdrew, leaving her missing his warmth. To take her mind off it, she ducked through the opening and stepped down into Stromberg's lair.

To her right, a velvet-upholstered theater seat folded down from the wall. A telephone had been mounted beside it, directly across from the portrait-door. Beneath the phone, a shelf held a neat row of black notebooks. The room was small enough that Nemo could reach out and touch the walls on both sides. Walls padded and covered with a lush brocade fabric to dampen sounds.

"He can sit here and do all his dirty-work in secret comfort." She chuckled. "Can't you picture him here, cataloging his misdeeds while he pets his fluffy cat?"

Aleksy leaned through the entrance. "Or a snake. Or an owl. But only predators. He would enjoy feeding them helpless prey. He is scum."

Nisha plucked the first book off the shelf and flipped it open to the first page. "Then let's find the proof we need to put him behind bars."

The leather-bound ledger contained lists of monetary transactions, dated, color-coded, and written in precise columns, but with no explanations for the meaning of the colors. Nisha scanned the names that topped each page, recognizing none of them. Every entry on the first dozen or so pages dated back to autumn of 1888.

She shoved the book back into place and reached for the furthest volume. Several dates in 1891 and 1892 jumped out at her. Perfect.

"I've got something. Let's take a look at this."

Nemo stepped back through the portrait into the office and laid the book open on the desk. The others gathered around, and they peered silently at the pages as Nemo flipped.

"Stop!" Alesky blurted.

Nemo froze.

Aleksy pointed at the name in curling script at the top of the page. "The soap man."

J. S. Simpson, 5 Sept. '91, the entry said, in green ink. Beneath it, a list penned in blue ran down the page, listing payments and dates spanning several months. The final payment was marked in red, with a date of March 16th of this year. Beside it was the date *29 May '92* in black.

"These are the payments to his minions," Victor said.

Mary nodded. "It looks like some sort of beginning date, end date, and all the payments made."

Callie rocked her baby, giving the girl a pat on the back. "I told you he would have it all in order."

Aleksy scrambled for the secret room. "I'll get the other books. We can look for all the names we recognize. See if we find others we know."

Nemo returned to flipping pages, scanning the names. *Stone, Dinsdale, Clay, Fortescue...*

"Let me see that," Mary interrupted.

Nisha handed her the book, and she turned back one page. *Augustus Clay.*

"That's my bastard of a late husband." Mary jabbed at the paper so hard her nail left a mark. "November 3rd of 1891. That must be when Stromberg made his deal with Clay. Then all the payments he made, and—" She dropped the book with a cry of alarm and whirled to bury her face against Victor's chest.

"Love, what's wrong?" Victor hugged her and smoothed a hand over her hair. "Are you able to tell us?"

Nisha retrieved the book and found the relevant page. Aleksy climbed out from the secret room, the other volumes in his arms, and came to stand next to her.

"The d-date at the end," Mary gasped, keeping her face hidden. "It's not a payment end date. The black date is... is the day Augustus was m-murdered."

Five voices swore in three different languages.

Nisha and Aleksy examined the book together, returning to Simpson's page and scanning slowly. Some names had nothing beneath the blue payments, but others like Simpson and Clay had a red date and a black date.

"Red is payment to the murderer," Nemo guessed. "Black is when the deed is done. I think this might be exactly what we need. Let's close up the secret room and leave at once."

Before shutting the book, she thumbed through to the most recent entries, wincing at the number of red and black dates. When she hit the last entry, her heart nearly stopped.

N. Majhi, 19 Apr. '92. The date Stomberg had offered to be her patron. No blue payments followed, since she'd never returned with the results of her submarine journey.

But there, beneath her name, in red ink, was written, *26 Jun. '92, $2000.*

Captain Nemo had a price on her head.

Chapter 27

Captain's Log, 8 July, 1892
A good crewmate will tell you what you need to hear.

Aleksy extracted the notebook from Nisha's trembling hand. "This goes to the police. Now."

He tucked all the books under one arm and began setting the room to rights. Close the portrait door. Push the stool back. Wheel the trash bin to the closet. Go, go, go.

He couldn't stop, not even for a moment. He had to move. Had to protect her. If he could put all his focus into that goal, he might be able to hold off the panic clawing at his chest.

Nemo snapped back into captain mode. "Aleksy and I will go straight to my father. The rest of you return to Victor's to hide. Stromberg knows all of us, so no one can assume they are safe. Stay out of sight. I'll phone after we consult with my father."

The others looked at one another, seeming to pass around some unspoken communication, but they didn't protest Nemo's orders.

Aleksy blew out a relieved breath. Good. He wanted her friends safe. She didn't need worries for them atop the worry for herself.

And at the moment, she was terrified. Her captain's

demeanor helped, he was sure, but it couldn't erase the small crinkles in her usually smooth brow or the tiny tick in her jaw. The faintest shimmer moistened her gorgeous dark eyes. She needed a hug.

But first, safety.

As swiftly as possible, Aleksy stored everything where it belonged, locked all the doors, and led everyone from the building. Once outside, they kept to the darkest areas of the streets until they were several blocks away.

Victor was the one to lift a hand and call a halt. "We're taking Hal and Callie and the baby to the bunker. Nemo, go straight to your father and be careful."

"Thank you for exactly restating my plan," she retorted.

"We'll be in touch," Victor continued, as if not hearing her. "I'm trusting your boy Szekalski to take care of you. You know we love you."

"I love you all too," she replied. "Don't worry about me. Aleksy is a fierce warrior."

A fierce warrior? She'd said it with as much easy confidence as she might have said "Aleksy is Polish" or "Aleksy is human." He stared after her, dazed, only belatedly realizing that she'd started down the road away from her friends.

Clutching the notebooks to his chest, he jogged to catch up and fell into step with her rapid strides.

"I'm fierce?"

She glanced at him, but the dim gaslight obscured her expression. "Of course you are. You are a man of convictions. Strong and steady and honorable. I can always rely on you. You're Aleksy Szekalski, Defender of All Creatures, Great and Small."

Aleksy suddenly didn't care that Nisha's face was in shadow. He didn't need to see her. He could hear everything in her voice. Admiration. Affection. Trust.

His heart began to race. All night he'd been counseling himself to have patience. To find a calm, rational moment to confess his love. A gentleman wouldn't burden his lady with selfish sentiment at a time like this. A gentleman would wait.

His brain, however, was no gentleman. With each second that passed, with each footfall on the pavement, it screamed louder. *Now, now, NOW.*

Aleksy fought the pounding in his head. He thought about the smooth leather of the books in his hands. One foot in front of the other, he marched down the street, taking the evidence to the police. Taking Nisha to safety. Still, the refrain continued on.

Now.

Now.

"I need to tell you something."

Damn.

He was only human. If she loved him—and he suspected she did—she would forgive his failure in this. Even fierce warriors had weaknesses, and Nisha was his.

Her steps slowed. "This had better not be some dire confession of all your past misdeeds because you think you're going to die."

"I— I beg your pardon?"

"No? Good." Nemo glanced over her shoulder. "We're not being followed, are we?"

"I don't think so." How much further was her home? Five blocks? Six? Why couldn't he have simply waited? "This is about us. Me."

She faltered. "Go on."

Aleksy drew closer to her, and together they resumed their brisk pace. Prickles of anxiety flowed through every nerve of his body, but he pressed forward.

"This adventure with you, I know it has been sometimes

scary. And sometimes peaceful and ordinary. But it is very special to me. I think when I fell onto your submarine and you looked down at me, something happened. Something magic."

Already he was rambling, the way he had about the cephalopods. And the copepods. And the axolotl. It was his nature. His thoughts came one atop another, like newspapers from a printing press, and his mouth did its best to keep up. Nisha never complained. Maybe she even liked it.

"You gave me a place to study life," Aleksy pressed on. "To follow my passion. You listened when I talked too much and gave me peace when I was silent. You shared your stories and asked about mine. You were the captain of your own ship, needing no crew, yet I became crew. Maybe more than crew. Maybe a partner. We worked well together." He patted the notebooks he held. "We *work* well together. Now. Maybe always."

Nisha's hand settled on his arm. "Yes. We are good together."

Hot tingles of desire joined the nervous fluttering in his belly. If his hands hadn't been full of precious evidence, he would have twined their fingers together. Perhaps kissed her knuckles.

"You cause me heart palpitations and shortness of breath," he whispered. "You are so exciting I am almost afraid."

Her beautiful laughter danced through the night air. "That is the most adorably unromantic romantic thing I've ever heard." She squeezed his arm and her voice became almost breathless. "Tell me more. Please."

This was it. His time to confess. He needed only to say the words.

"Last night, on the submarine, do you remember?" It

seemed so long ago. Those perfect moments. The heartbreak when he thought she didn't want him. Her mumbled words were clearer now. That moment had marked an end. And she hadn't known he wanted it to be a beginning.

"How could I forget?" she asked. "It was spectacular."

"I said words to you. 'Kocham Cię.'" Aleksy stopped walking and turned fully toward her. He wanted to see her face when he told her. "I didn't tell you what it means. But I had to say it. You were so beautiful. You belonged in my arms. Kocham Cię, Nisha Majhi. In Engli—"

She shoved him, hard, and he stumbled backward, nearly losing his balance. An object clattered on the pavement, but Aleksy's brain couldn't process what or why. Nemo yanked one of the notebooks from his hands and flung it like a discus. Behind him a man yelped in pain.

Aleksy whirled around, his senses belatedly surging to full alert.

Danger! Protect her!

The man who had cried out stood half in shadow, one hand clutched to his face. The book Nisha had thrown at him lay splayed on the ground at his feet. The villain fumbled to pry something from his wide belt. The movement brought him further into the light, displaying a row of gleaming throwing knives.

"Run!" Aleksy shielded Nisha's body with his own, propelling her forward. "Run!"

Another knife clanged on the ground. A bad throw. The man was still disoriented. But he wouldn't be for long.

Aleksy sprinted down the road, glued to Nemo's side, braced to take a knife in the back to keep her from harm. The streets ahead grew brighter as the gas lamps gave way to the arc lights of her family's neighborhood. Fewer shadows. No place to hide.

Nisha veered around a corner. "We can't lead them home," she panted. "The submarine. We need to get back to the submarine."

It would be a long run. But the footsteps of their pursuer were fading fast. They could make it. Regroup. Use the telegraph to notify the police.

The chug of a steam engine and the rumble of tires over cobblestones dashed Aleksy's hopes. Already his legs were tiring. No man could outrun a steam car for more than a matter of seconds.

Nisha made an abrupt one hundred eighty degree turn, grabbing Aleksy's jacket to pull him with her. He fumbled the books, nearly dropped one, and lost all his momentum in the process. The approaching steam car turned the corner, heading straight for them.

"Follow me!" Nemo shouted.

Aleksy didn't hesitate. When the captain had an idea, it was usually a good one. Squinting in the glare from the enemy's headlights, he tore down the sidewalk after her, clutching the notebooks even tighter than before. He would not lose her and he would not lose the evidence. He was her warrior and he would walk through hell before betraying her faith in him.

Boots pounding on the sidewalk, they ran right past the oncoming vehicle. Tires squealed as their pursuers tried to turn around, but the tactic had given Aleksy and Nisha a few precious seconds. Perhaps enough to hide, if not run.

"Home," Nisha gasped, clutching her side as she ran. "Dadi's car."

Her grandmother's prototype? Mrs. Majhi had said it was fast. And if anyone could escape an enemy in a vehicle still undergoing testing, it would be Captain Nemo.

But, dammit, he still hadn't professed his feelings for her. Well, he wasn't waiting another godforsaken second.

Aleksy sucked in the deepest breath he could and shouted, "I love you, Nisha!"

Chapter 28

Captain's Log, 8 July, 1892
A good crewmate will know when to disobey orders.

The lights inside Franklin Castle burned low in the pre-dawn hours, but Victor didn't need them to read the expression on Hal's face. It exactly matched his own. Serious. Determined.

Victor gave a slight nod to Hal, Callie, and the baby. "You three will be safe in the bunker. Use the telephone there and call everyone you can think of. The police, the newspapers, the Pinkertons, the local bowling club, I don't care. If you think they might be able to help, call them. Tell everyone."

"I'll do it," Hal replied.

Callie touched his arm affectionately. "And I'll help you so nothing goes wrong."

Victor almost smiled at that. Hal's hatred of machines ran deep, but his loyalty to Nemo would outweigh it any day.

"Thank you both," Victor said. "We'll go after Nemo and her beau and make certain they're safe."

Mary touched the shoulder of the metal man that stood between her and Victor. "And take Mech along to provide extra protection."

"Take care." Hal extended a hand to Victor and the two

men clasped forearms in their old college tradition. "In Scientific Solidarity."

"Solidarity," Victor repeated.

The Mad Scientists Society had only three members, but they took care of their own. While Hal and Victor drew breath, Nemo would never face a murderer alone.

Victor locked the house securely and notified the night watchman to be on extra alert before climbing into his car with Mary and Mecha-Man. Nemo's house wasn't far from his own, but the stop to drop off Hal and Callie and pick up Mech had put them well behind. Victor accelerated to an illegally fast speed, determined to make up as much time as possible.

"They will be fine." Mary's comforting touch trailed down his arm. "Nisha knows how to be cautious, and I believe Mr. Szekalski cares deeply for her."

Victor didn't doubt it. As a man desperately in love himself, he recognized the signs. "Szekalski would wrestle a shark before letting anyone so much as scratch her. It's the only reason I let them go off alone in the first place."

"First. Place," Mecha-Men echoed. "You. Win."

"I sincerely hope we do," Victor replied. He tilted his head toward Mary. "Idioms still unrecognized. Could you remind me to jot that down when we return home?"

Squealing tires cut off her answer.

Victor cursed and spun the wheel in the direction of the noise. If that was anything other than some feckless youth playing with daddy's car…

A gleaming car barreled through the intersection some fifty yards ahead of them, followed seconds later by another vehicle. Victor yanked on the brake, bringing his car to a shuddering halt. They'd do Nemo no good by colliding with an enemy.

"Fuck." He flicked his headlights off. "They beat us, and now they're after her. Do you hear any others?"

He listened intently, but the only sound he could make out was the dwindling rumble of the two racing cars. He reached for the throttle. They'd give chase.

Mary's hand clamped down on his. Victor went absolutely still. A *bump* echoed down the street, like a tire bouncing over a rut. A moment later he caught the murmur of spinning wheels and the subtle hiss of steam.

He held his breath as the car rolled past. All black and with no lights, inside or out, it drifted by like a wraith in the darkness.

Stromberg.

Victor would have bet his life on it. That black car belonged to the villain in the shadows. The man behind the curtain. Waiting. Watching. Stalking. Nemo would elude her pursuer, but Stromberg would steal through the darkness, looking for an opportunity to strike. When the last of his minions failed, he would do the deed himself.

"We need to split up," Victor gasped. "We need the police *now*. Send them to the submarine. I'll follow that car."

Mary's fingers dug into his arm so tightly it hurt. "I am not leaving you."

"But we…"

She silenced him with a wave and turned to face Mecha-Man. "Mech, do you remember when we practiced with the map?"

"Map. Yes," the metal man replied.

"Good. Now I want you to listen very carefully and do exactly as I say."

Mech nodded. "Yes, Mama."

Chapter 29

Captain's Log, 8 July, 1892
Good crewmates learn to communicate with one another.

Good gods, the torque! This new prototype of Dadi's was an absolute beast. The rate of acceleration stole Nemo's breath and flattened her against the seat. She clung to the steering wheel. This car would do wonders in the hands of an expert. In the hands of a woman accustomed to driving a submarine, it was one wrong twitch from disaster.

She careened around a corner, praying she was guessing correctly about the speed and the handling.

The tires skidded over the pavement. Too fast.

"Dammit!" Trying to adjust, Nemo yanked on the wheel, but overcorrected and sent the car into a bouncing zig-zag. "Shit!"

The car lurched down the road as she wrangled it back under control. Blast it all, they would never outrun their enemies this way.

"I'm sorry!" she called over the rush of wind. Why did these fast cars never have roofs? Couldn't they be made with a nice curved hull for proper aerodynamics, like her *Narwhal*?

Aleksy answered with a nod, not looking at her. He knelt

backwards on the seat beside her, watching the car behind while she drove. Navigator to her pilot, once again.

Nisha whizzed around another corner, taking this turn with a fraction more finesse than before. She gave a half-laugh. Only fifty or sixty more turns and she'd have it.

"We are a few more yards ahead," Aleksy reported.

Sweat slicked her palms. She needed to push this car to its limits if they were to escape. If only her body weren't a knotted ball of tension. But Stromberg wanted her dead, someone was chasing her, she'd been up all night, and Aleksy was sitting right next to her and he'd said he loved her.

The memory of that moment couldn't quite penetrate her focus on the road. Had it even really happened? Had he truly shouted those words while they ran down the street?

"That's all you have to say, then?" she demanded.

"What?"

"You tell me you love me and then not a word?" Another corner. Easier this time. The talking kept her from over-thinking.

"I... what word?" Aleksy turned to look at her and reached up to touch his ear. "It's hard to hear."

"You love me!" Nisha shouted. She would be reporting to her grandmother that this car made too much noise at high speed.

"Yes!" he yelled back. "I do!"

"And?"

"And what?"

Nemo gritted her teeth and opened up the throttle. If they could get some separation along this long, straight section, maybe they could finally shake off the other car.

"You can't say you love me and then say nothing!"

Aleksy resumed watching behind them. "We're pulling ahead. Go faster!" He gripped the back of the seat with both hands. "I said nothing because you didn't reply!" he added. "Turn left!"

"That's away from the river! And excuse me for—"

"We can circle Cadillac Square and turn around!"

"—being distracted!" Nemo wrenched the wheel, pleading with every one of the gods that this wouldn't kill them both. "Fuck, fuck, and triple fuck!"

The car skidded around the bend, jittered a bit, then settled.

Aleksy twisted completely around until he was seated in a normal position. "When you save us, I'll give you all the fucking you want."

"How can you—" The car hit a bit of debris in the road and bounced, jolting her nearly out of her seat. "—joke at a time like this?"

Aleksy checked behind them, then gently touched her shoulder. "It's the only way I can protect you now."

More of his earlier words sprang to mind. *Magic. Together. Always.* Always caring. Always there for her. The unrelenting wind caught the tears that welled in her eyes, dragging wet trails across her cheeks.

He turned his mouth toward her ear. "I would die for you, Nisha-mine."

"No." Nisha pushed her shoulders back and straightened her spine. She swung the car around the curve at the eastern end of the square, then yanked it into a sharp left, using the pedestrian pathway to cut diagonally across the park. "No one is dying! You are not leaving me."

The steam car bounced and rattled over the narrow dirt path, but her grandmother's design did the family proud. It lurched back onto the roadway at the opposite end of the park, leaving the enemy's lesser ride in the dust.

"We are crewmates," Nemo continued. "And that means

we sail as a team! How could I go anywhere without my navigator?"

She started the car on a circuitous route toward the docks. After several more turns, she slowed to a pace better suited to stealth. No more sounds of chasing cars drifted through the still air. Instead, waking birds chirped the arrival of dawn. Off to the east, a soft purple glow pushed away the blackness of night. To the south, red and green dots announced the departure of early-morning sailors. Her submarine awaited.

Nisha brought the car to a halt beside the dockyard. Her hair was a tangled mess, and her eyes stung from the wind and the tears. When she spoke, her voice was hoarse from shouting.

"I couldn't reply then, but I'm replying now. I love your heart, Aleksy Szekalski. I love your bravery and your loyalty. You protect everyone, Mr. Sexy-Warrior-Scientist." She placed a hand to his chest, feeling the steady heartbeat beneath his shirt. "But, damn it all, I get to protect you too. I don't want to live in a world that doesn't have you in it. I love you and I want to explore the world with you until we're both old and gray and our great-grandchildren are the ones building submarines and discovering new species!"

He skimmed his fingers across her cheek, then down to trace her lips. "Aye, aye, Captain," he murmured, and kissed her.

Nisha's entire body went slack with relief. Aleksy's mouth moved over hers in tender, feather-light sweeps, each gentle caress a promise.

"Kocham Cię," he whispered. A kiss. "I love you." Another kiss. "You are finer than treasure."

She twined her arms around his neck, sliding her tongue between his lips to deepen the kiss. He embraced her in response, hauling her half out of her seat to bring their bodies together.

All gentleness vanished from the kiss. Every ounce of love erupted from her heart, wild and fierce, full of fire and power. Aleksy equalled her passion in every way, unafraid of the force of her love, willing to combust with her. Her ideal partner.

I love you.

Nisha's mouth was too preoccupied to say the words aloud, but they sang in her head like a choir. She used her body to communicate instead. Her lips and tongue made a thorough perusal of his mouth, savoring every texture and taste. Her arms tightened around him, pressing his chest into her heavy, aching breasts. Every part of her strained to be closer to him, wanting, needing. Now. Always.

A patronizing chuckle cut through the haze of desire, causing both Nemo and Aleksy to flinch.

"Well, well, what sweet little lovebirds together in their nest," a malevolent voice jeered.

Nemo's head whipped around to meet the triumphant gaze of Talon Stromberg.

Her enemy lifted a pistol and aimed it straight at her heart. "Pity they never saw the eagle swooping down until he had them in his claws."

Chapter 30

Captain's Log, 8 July, 1892
The crew is by far the most valuable part of any ship.

Aleksy needed every ounce of his willpower not to launch himself out of the car at Stromberg. This was not the time to take a bullet. Not when Nisha had declared only minutes ago that she intended them to grow old together.

"Idź do diabła, ty cholerna świnio," he snarled.

Stromberg chuckled. "Such colorful language. Russian?"

"Polish, you piece of dogshit."

Nisha squeezed Aleksy's arm to quiet him, but no captain's command would sway him. He wanted Stromberg's attention on him, not her. And he wanted to keep the man talking.

"Your lover is rather hostile, Miss Majhi." Stromberg patted a canvas bag that he wore slung across his body. It bulged out in the middle, but at this time of day the lighting wasn't good enough for Aleksy to guess at the shape inside. "Aggressive. Perhaps he is more a predator than I thought. Or is he only roused in defense of his mate?"

"What do you want, Stromberg?" Nisha demanded.

Her body trembled, even as she forced strength into her words. Aleksy kept himself pressed close to her, conveying as much love and support as he could while facing down an armed villain.

"You must know you've lost," Nisha continued. "Your minions have failed, your plans have been uncovered. What do you hope to accomplish? Petty revenge?"

"I've lost?" Stromberg guffawed. "You must be joking. I have many remaining options, and despite your bluster, you have no evidence against me."

Thank God Stromberg was looking at Nemo, or he might have noticed Aleksy's gaze drop for a split second. The notebooks they'd stolen from the secret room sat on the floor of the car at his feet. Keeping his movements as small as possible, Aleksy nudged the books beneath the seat and out of view. Whatever happened, the police would find this car and the proof they needed.

Stromberg waggled his gun. "What I want now, Miss Majhi, is your submarine. You have shown beyond a doubt that it is the vehicle I need for my future ventures. Its speed, stealth, and maneuverability allow it to evade any surface ship. Add a few weapons, and I will be unstoppable."

"The *Narwhal* will never carry weapons," she spat.

"Ah, my dear girl, it's such a pity your great talents lie in so soft a heart. I should have expected it of a woman."

"Kindness is not weakness," Aleksy retorted, trying again to draw Stromberg's focus away from Nisha. "And the captain has a heart of fire. She will burn you to ash."

Stromberg swung the pistol slowly from Nisha to Aleksy. "Take me to the submarine, Miss Majhi. Or I will silence your insolent brat of a lover permanently."

Nisha kicked the car door open, causing Stromberg to skitter backward to avoid being struck. She stepped down to the ground and jabbed a finger toward the docks. "The ship is that way."

What? Aleksy scrambled out of the car after her. Stromberg would have a clearer shot at him now, but what choice was there? Nisha appeared to have some plan, and he couldn't abandon her.

"Do you think me a fool, girl?" Stromberg scoffed. "I know I can't board the ship on my own. And I have no training on how to pilot it. You will take me aboard and teach me your controls, or your paramour will die."

Nemo folded her arms over her chest and glared. Despite her outer disdain, Aleksy spied hints of her inner fear. A slight tic in her jaw. A sheen in the corner of one beautiful, dark eye. A bit of a hunch to her shoulders.

"Let Mr. Szekalski leave unharmed, and I will show you to the submarine," she replied.

Damnation. This was not happening. She wouldn't surrender her ship. Not her beloved submarine. It was her life's work. Her hope and dream for the future. No, no, absolutely not.

"He comes with us," Stromberg insisted, adjusting his aim. "Otherwise how can I trust that you will do as you say?"

"How can we trust you won't kill us when you have what you want?" Aleksy shot back.

"I am a man of business. I understand the importance of contractual obligations. When the ship is fully mine, you will be free to go."

Free to wander into the hands of a paid assassin.

"To the submarine, boy, before I relieve you of a limb or two to display my sincerity."

Nisha nudged Aleksy. "Go."

The stricken expression on her face said everything. She truly was willing to give up her ship to keep him safe. Her firm denial when he'd told her he would die for her suddenly made perfect sense. He didn't want her to sacrifice every-thing for him. He wanted to see her flourish. To have the life she deserved. And she wanted the same for him.

Aleksy's rage at Stromberg flared higher, and his muscles tensed, ready to spring into action and pummel the man.

Nie. No. Not now.

He started for the submarine, Nemo at his side. To keep his impulsive nature in check, he concentrated on his sur-roundings: the ground beneath his feet, the slight breeze off the river, Stromberg's steady footfalls behind him. Every one of his senses needed to be at high alert.

Hold back, hold back. The time will come.

An opportunity would present itself, and when it did, he would give in to his instincts. He wouldn't let the bastard hurt his beloved. Not now, not ever.

During the walk to where the *Narwhal* was moored, Aleksy contemplated at least a dozen ways to kill or incapac-itate Stromberg. None were practical. He had no weapons, no training. His only dangerous skills were his ability to throw a punch and his finesse with a kitchen knife. The chances of retrieving a knife without getting shot were slim. Getting in a punch was more likely, but it would require Stromberg to be thoroughly distracted.

Nemo unlocked the hatch, then twisted and turned several things to open it. Lights inside clicked on. Stromberg craned his neck to peer down, but didn't approach.

"You first, Miss Majhi. Then the boy. Wait by the bottom of the ladder until I am aboard. We wouldn't want any trouble at this stage, now would we?"

Nisha looked her enemy in the eye. "If you harm Aleksy, I will sink you to the bottom of the river."

Stromberg shook his head. "Cooperate, and I will have no need to harm him."

Nisha gave Aleksy a stern look, a silent warning not to try anything. Perhaps she didn't realize that her captain's orders no longer worked on him. If he obeyed her, it would be because they were in a position where her skills and knowledge made her the best choice to lead. But she no longer outranked him. They were partners and he would choose when to trust his own judgment. Sometimes they would disagree, perhaps even quarrel. But he would never, ever, stop defending her, even if she was defending him right back.

She dropped down into the submarine. Aleksy followed, taking two steps toward the galley before he stopped himself. There wasn't time to get a knife.

Wait for your chance. Keep him distracted.

Stromberg landed at the bottom of the ladder, pistol still in hand. "Excellent. You may close the hatch, Miss Majhi."

"On this ship, you address her as Captain," Aleksy retorted. "If you think so highly of her submarine, you might at least have the decency to show her the proper respect."

Nemo threw him a furious look. "Enough," she hissed. "I do *not* want him to shoot you." She turned to Stromberg. "The helm is this way."

Aleksy clenched his fists. No, it wasn't enough. Stromberg remained focused and confident. They needed him off-balance.

Nisha strode leisurely to the helm, her pace far slower than her usual business-like stride. Stalling for time? Good. Perhaps the others had already been in contact with the police. Perhaps Nisha's father would think to send people to guard the submarine. Perhaps someone had spotted Stromberg's gun and had run for help.

Aleksy didn't know how likely any of those scenarios were, but Nemo's delaying tactics gave him an extra burst of hope. Yes, she would sacrifice her ship to save him, but she wouldn't do it without a fight.

"This, here, is the control for the hatch." She waved a hand at a lever on the control panel as if giving a tour to a sightseer. "While it can be closed manually, similarly to the way I opened it, using the pneumatic system allows for a more powerful pull than even an exceptional human could accomplish. This leads to a tighter seal and greater protection against leakage."

Stromberg gave her a nod. "Good. Close it."

Nemo grasped the lever. "Operation is simple. Push away from you to close, pull toward you to open."

The lever wasn't hard to move. Aleksy had seen her operate it with hardly a flick of her wrist. This time, however, she gave it a slow, steady push. The mechanism clicked.

"If you listen, you can hear the hiss of the hatch closing."

To Aleksy's surprise, Stromberg cocked an ear toward the hatch and said nothing. Did he not realize that Nisha was stalling, or was he so confident that he didn't care?

From this distance, the hissing of the pneumatics almost disappeared into the background noise. The *clank* when the hatch settled into place, however, echoed through the ship's metal body like a thunderclap.

Stromberg flinched, and for a second his grip on the pistol faltered. Aleksy rocked forward, but before he could take a full step, Stomberg recovered.

Drat. So close.

The slip showed Stromberg could be distracted, though. All Aleksy needed was the right moment.

Nemo continued with her delaying tactic. "Once the hatch is fully closed, I make a check of the diagnostic gauges on this part of the panel. Oxygen levels. Air pressure. Inside temperature. Outside temperature. Outside pressure." She touched each gauge as she spoke. "If anything was abnormal, we would abort any mission immediately."

Stromberg›s smug smile had morphed into a scowl. His gaze roved between Aleksy and Nisha. He took aim with his pistol. "Do not forget, Miss Majhi."

"You don't want to shoot me in here," Aleksy challenged. If he could get Stromberg arguing, perhaps they could delay in a different fashion. As long as they remained at the surface, they had a chance. "The bullet could do damage to the submarine. Or it could bounce off all the metal and fly back at you."

Stromberg neither argued nor scoffed. A grin so broad it was almost boyish lit his face. He pocketed the gun and reached into his bag. "I need no gun."

Aleksy took a step backward. What was in there? A bomb? A deadly poison?

Stromberg lifted a thick coiled rope from the bag. A scaly rope that wriggled and made a low, growling hiss.

Fuck.

The cobra flared its hood when Stromberg held it aloft. "Meet my friend," the villain crooned. "A highly lethal species. Its venom—"

Bang! Bang! Bang!

The sound reverberated through the hull. Thanks to previous incidents, Aleksy knew immediately the noise came from outside the ship. Someone knew they were inside. Friend? Or foe?

Tink. Bang! Bang! Tink.

Aleksy's heart leapt. Morse code again. The delay had worked. Help had arrived!

Tink.

O-P-E. The next noise would be a dash-dot. N. Open up.

"Take this ship down, girl," Stromberg snarled. He

pointed the snake's head at Aleksy. "This cobra's venom can kill a man in half an hour. The bite will first cause extreme pain and blurred vision. Then your body will begin to fail. Your muscles will become paralyzed. Your heart may give out. Even if it doesn't, your lungs will cease to function and you will perish from asphyxiation."

Stromberg took a step toward Aleksy, holding the snake at arm's length. He made no attempt to support the animal, letting it dangle from his fist. The cobra writhed, trying to break loose. Stromberg, though, had an iron grip. The snake twisted and contorted, straining for freedom, but to no avail.

That bastard! He was hurting the poor thing. No wonder it was angry. It had every right to feel threatened and defensive.

The snake let out a loud, furious hiss.

Don't worry. I'll save you, Aleksy promised. *I'll save Nisha and the submarine and you, and I won't let that pestilent scum harm anyone ever again. Somehow.*

The rhythmic banging continued overhead, joined by clunks and scrapes in no discernible pattern. Were their rescuers trying to pry the hatch open?

Delay, delay, delay.

"Don't be afraid," Aleksy soothed the snake, though he knew the animal couldn't hear him. "I won't hurt you."

Stromberg turned to Nisha with a snarl. "Take this ship down." He flung the snake at Aleksy's feet.

The cobra reared up, its hood wide, poised to strike.

"Now."

Chapter 31

Captain's Log, 8 July, 1892
Trust your crew to help you make decisions. Two heads are
better than one.

Nisha froze when the snake raised its head and emitted another chilling growl.

Manasa, protect us. Let this snake be of the Naga, come to bite only the truly evil.

The snake turned its head slowly from side to side, not seeming to fixate on any particular target. Nisha glanced at Aleksy for assistance. He understood animals. Of everyone she knew, he would be best equipped to face a deadly creature.

Like her, he had gone completely still. Unlike her, his posture was relaxed, almost fearless. He knew something.

Nemo reached for the controls to begin their descent. Giving in to Stromberg's demands made her sick, both in body and heart, but right now it was imperative that she prevent him doing anything worse to Aleksy or prodding the cobra into attacking. More delaying.

The *Narwhal* responded as she always did, smooth and sure. If only she knew she and her crew were under threat. She would fight for their freedom.

The banging outside ceased as water began to creep up

the window. Their allies would need to scramble back onto the pier.

Nisha looked back at Aleksy. The snake showed no interest in him, though it still wiggled and hissed. When she dropped her hand from the controls, it paused, looking in her direction.

She caught Aleksy's eye, giving him a questioning look. *What do I do?*

He held her gaze for a moment, then looked down at the snake, then back up at her. Only his eyes moved.

Aha! He wanted her to hold completely still. She could do that. The cobra must be sensitive to movement.

Keeping her head as still as possible, she glanced at Stromberg. He was watching the rising water, a triumphant smile on his face.

"Thank you, Miss Majhi, for my ship. I assume once we are submerged I can use the wheel to steer us away from the dock and into deeper waters?" He didn't wait for an answer. "I must admit, it is gratifying to have someone to witness my victory. Running everything from the shadows does have its advantages, but it can become tiresome."

Stromberg slowly lifted a hand to the control panel. His fingers caressed the smooth metal, circling buttons and switches.

Nemo choked down a sudden upwelling of bile. How dare he? How dare he touch this ship with his soiled fingers? How dare he defile her with his poisonous lust?

Nisha's gaze shot back to Aleksy. Enraged. Determined. They needed to stop this.

Help me. We can't let him do this.

"My lovely pet," Stromberg crooned. He stroked the submarine's controls as if she were a furry animal in his lap.

"How sleek and stealthy you are. Just think how glorious you will be when I have given you teeth."

Only a stern look from Aleksy prevented Nisha from moving. He looked pointedly down at the snake, then at Stromberg. When Aleksy's gaze returned to hers, he wiggled his eyes up and down and side-to-side in no apparent pattern.

Snake, him, move. Nemo gave Aleksy the slightest of nods. She needed to get Stromberg to move. Make the snake chase him. Even a step or two backward would put him as close to the cobra as Aleksy was. He couldn't steal her ship if he was running for his life.

Nisha dropped her own gaze to the control panel, then lifted her hand inch by agonizing inch.

"And there we are," Stromberg crowed, as the water passed the top of the windows. "Fully submerged." His hand drifted toward the steering wheel.

With the tiniest flick of her finger, Nisha flipped the open-hatch switch.

The klaxon horn screeched. Emergency lights flashed red and yellow. Stromberg let out a cry and leapt back from the controls.

The cobra struck.

Stromberg roared in shock and pain as the snake sank its fangs into the meatiest part of his calf. "Help!" He flailed at the cobra, but the animal jerked away as quickly as it had struck, then scurried out the door into the depths of the submarine.

Aleksy dove at Stromberg, knocking him to the floor and wrestling the pistol from his pocket. An instant later, Aleksy was back on his feet, weapon aimed at the enemy.

Stromberg didn't rise. The venom he'd raved about had gone to work, and his body no longer responded to his commands. He writhed and whimpered. There would be no pompous last words.

Ah-ooh-ga! Ah-oog-ga!

Nemo pushed the hatch control to "close," shutting off the alarms. She reversed the descent, then gave her *Narwhal* an affectionate pat.

"That's my girl. No bad man will hurt you now."

"Or harm my captain," Aleksy snarled. He held the pistol with both hands, and Nemo had no doubt he would pull the trigger if Stromberg showed even a sign of recovering.

"Or the captain's mate," Nemo declared, equally fervently. They *would* have a future together. She would see to it.

By the time the *Narwhal* was fully surfaced, Stromberg had ceased moving. What had he said? Paralysis and respiratory failure? From the look of things, he was quite possibly beyond help.

Aleksy waved Nisha up the hatch first. "Go. I have the gun and can stay safe from the snake if it appears."

She scrambled up the ladder, only to have a pair of hands grab each arm and haul her through the hatch. Her yelp cut off as she recognized Mary and Victor.

"Where's that scoundrel?" Victor demanded.

Aleksy, who must have heard her aborted cry of alarm, popped up through the hatch, pistol first. Victor lunged.

"Whoa!" Nisha jumped between them, throwing both hands in the air. "All friends here!"

The two men fell back when recognition set in.

"Dzięki Bogu," Aleksy gasped, at the same time Victor blurted, "Thank God."

The squeal of car tires announced a new arrival. A black car marked with the emblem of the Detroit Police drove right off the road and bounced over grass and gravel nearly to the dock. A door flew open and Nisha's father leapt out. Mecha-Man lumbered from the opposite side.

"Mama. Papa." The metal man waved.

More police cars swarmed in behind them, and officers spilled out, guns and nightsticks at the ready.

"Police," Mecha-Man declared.

"Atta-boy, Mech!" Victor cheered.

Nisha's father ran toward her, and she flew into his embrace.

"Nisha, my baby," he crooned.

"I'm fine, Baba. I'm safe." She hugged him fiercely, then drew back and pointed at the hatch. "Stromberg is down there. He was bitten by a cobra, and I don't know how much longer he has to live. We have proof that he was the villain behind all the Sobridyne poisonings."

"It's safe in the car," Aleksy added. "Nisha's grandmother's car."

Her father stared at them, brows arched. "A cobra?"

"Stromberg is also an animal smuggler. His own cobra bit him and now it's loose on my ship."

"Mecha-Man can fetch the bastard for you, Chief." Victor gave his and Mary's creation a proud smile.

Nisha's father nodded. "Bring him up as fast as you can. Now what's this about proof?"

"We found his secret notebooks," she explained.

Her father's jaw tightened. "Do not tell me where or how."

"Oh, I found them while cleaning," Aleksy said with an impish smile. "I'm the janitor."

"I thought you were a biologist."

"Renowned," Nisha said firmly. "He discovered a new species of—Oh, shit. Not again."

That damned boat. That damned mauve-trimmed boat

was cruising into port, aiming for the empty place right beside her submarine.

She gestured at the incoming vessel. "That's Stromberg's ship." Had it escaped the pirates? Damn and double damn. The minions wouldn't know Stromberg lay dying. They'd come after her, hoping for that two thousand dollars.

Her father waved his men into action. "Watch that ship. Question everyone who disembarks."

"Ahoy!" a cheery voice called out. "Ahoy, Captain!"

Nisha blinked. She raised a hand to shield her eyes and peered out at the river. The light of the rising sun illuminated a man in sailor's garb standing at the prow of Stromberg's former craft. Beyond, just coming into view, was the *SS Audacity*.

"Ahoy, *Narwhal*!" Merriman shouted.

Nisha waved. "Hello!" She turned back to her father. "You can call off your men. It's only the pirates."

"Pirates?" He put a hand to his temple. "Nisha, you and your friends…"

She shrugged. "Well, we *are* Mad Scientists, after all."

Chapter 32

Captain's Log, 8 July, 1892
Good relationships are worth more than gold.

The pirates didn't look particularly fierce or dangerous. They hopped off the boat and secured it to the dock in exactly the same fashion any sailor would. They wore typical sailing attire and chatted good-naturedly as they worked. Aleksy had to admit his opinion of them was higher since their assistance.

The police didn't seem to think the pirates of any significance. Most of them had scrambled to their cars, escorting Stromberg's unconscious body to the hospital.

Aleksy hoped the bastard recovered enough to feel the consequences of his mistakes.

Chief Majhi directed half-a-dozen men into positions around Nisha and her friends. "Accompany my daughter and her companions wherever she decides to go," he instructed. "If there's any trouble, bring them to the station." He lifted the notebooks his men had retrieved from the car. "I'm taking these to headquarters, then I'll be at the hospital."

Nisha yawned, and Aleksy automatically took her arm to offer support. "We will go home soon. Captain Majhi needs rest."

Her father nodded. "Good. You can stay in our guest

room. You will both need to make a statement about this…
incident." He kissed Nisha on the cheek and departed.

"Let's see to the submarine and then get you to bed,"
Aleksy suggested.

"And you," she insisted. "You do not get to tuck me in
and then hover nearby like a dragon guarding treasure."

She was still trying to take care of him. Aleksy couldn't
help but grin. This was how their life would be. Looking
out for one another. Reminding each other that taking care
of oneself was as important as taking care of one's partner.
Helping one another thrive.

He couldn't wait to get started.

"But you *are* my treasure," he murmured. He leaned in
for a quick kiss, but a voice interrupted.

"Ah, Captain!" Merriman trotted toward them. "So glad
I found you. I need to consult with Dr. Szekalski."

"I'm not—"

"This is a lovely vessel," the pirate continued, waving
at his captured boat. "And I'm thrilled that I got the chance
to avenge myself against that son of a bitch. His damned
smugglers ruined the best whiskey run, then they shot up
one of my ships. We saved her—barely—but lost all our
cargo. But, now I've got a nice new addition to the fleet,
and he's… well, he didn't look too good when they carried
him out."

A brightly colored bird flew over from the direction of
Merriman's ship to land on the pirate's shoulder. It had a
squat, round body and a long, curved beak. Some variety
of toucan.

Merriman grimaced. "This. This is why I need the
biologist. That ship is crammed with animals. Birds, lizards,
giant insects, some strange furry thing that looks like a rat
mated with a rabbit. Lovely soft fur, though."

"Chinchilla?" Aleksy guessed.

"Ah, yes. That's it. And then this." The pirate gestured at the bird. "'Curl-crested aracari,' it said on the cage. The cage we can't get it back into. It just flies off, then only comes back to me. I don't know what to do with it."

"Feed it fruit," Aleksy suggested. "And let it eat the insects on the ship."

"Right. But I, uh…" Merriman removed his cap and ran a hand through his hair. "I don't have to keep them all, do I?"

"I'd be happy to help you find proper homes for all the animals. I will need to make a list of ethical scientists and zoological gardens who can care for them." The toucan squawked and Aleksy grinned. "In the meantime, it will be fun to see them and make sure they are properly fed and healthy." He bounced in place. He would have to make sure not to name them all, or he'd end up wanting to keep them, like Nadia.

"You could open an animal shelter." Nisha's voice was unusually soft, her gaze focused on the submarine.

They needed to get her home. This night had been interminable, and she'd nearly lost everything. Even if Aleksy couldn't curl up with her, like he wanted, he would be under the same roof, and that would be enough for now.

He wrapped an arm around her. "A shelter would be interesting, but I have no money."

Nisha didn't take her eyes off the *Narwhal*. "You have thirty percent of the gold."

Aleksy started. "What?"

She stepped away from his grasp and finally turned to look at him. "We found it together. Our share is half yours. You can take the money and do anything you like with it. So open a shelter. Go to college and get a degree if it makes you feel official. Join Merriam's crew and become a pirate pet sitter."

Aleksy's brow furrowed. If that was a joke, she hadn't delivered it with much humor. She wasn't smiling. And she was fidgeting with the bottom button of her vest. Cool Captain Nemo was nervous.

"Are we not going to explore the world together?" he asked.

"We can," she replied. She dropped her hands and shoved them into her pockets. "I meant it when I said I love you. That wasn't the danger of the car chase talking."

Merriman began to back away. "I'll go see about putting this fellow in his cage." The toucan flew up in the air, circled for a few moments, then landed on his other shoulder.

"Oh, I don't care if you know," Nisha sighed. "I don't care if any of you know." She gestured at Mary, Victor, and the nearby policemen.

"We definitely already knew," Victor said. His wife elbowed him.

"Yes," Nemo went on, her attention back to Aleksy. "I love you. I want you to join me and explore on the submarine. But I won't demand it. I made you stay, at the beginning, and that was wrong of me. I don't want a prisoner, an accidental stowaway, or a subordinate. I want a partner. And I want you to have a choice in the matter."

Aleksy stepped toward her, grasped her wrists and gently lifted her hands from her pockets. He kissed her knuckles. "That is also what I want. Nothing would make me happier. I choose you. I will always choose you." He leaned close and whispered, "Will you marry me?"

She beamed at him, eyes shimmering. "Are you willing to have a Hindu ceremony?"

"Of course. Are you willing to have a Catholic one?"

"Yes."

He kissed her—quickly, because they were in public, but with all the love in his heart.

"We will have two beautiful wedding ceremonies," he declared, now loud enough for everyone to hear. "And one huge party full of music, dancing, drinks, and food."

The pirates whistled and cheered.

Aleksy frowned at his beloved. "Do they think they're invited?"

Nemo shrugged. She opened her mouth to reply, only to be drowned out by the sound of yet another approaching car. She and Aleksy both turned to look, then swore simultaneously. The men who had chased them earlier had found them at last. And they'd brought friends.

Victor grabbed Nemo's arm. "We can hide in the submarine. Let the police handle them."

She shook herself free. "There's a deadly cobra on the submarine!"

Merriman cleared his throat. He made a series of hand signals toward his crew. They passed on the signals to the men up on Stromberg's former boat, who signaled to the *Audacity*.

The police officers pulled their guns when Stromberg's men stepped out of their vehicles.

Aleksy tugged Nisha toward the submarine. A cobra was far safer than a gunfight.

He didn't get far. A thunderous boom shook the entire pier, and a cannonball tore through one of the enemy steam cars.

The minions screamed in terror and ran, some limping

or clutching shrapnel wounds. The police raced after them. It was over. At last.

Nisha yanked Aleksy tight against her. "I'm exhausted. Let›s go home." She glanced at Merriman. "And the pirates are definitely invited to the wedding."

Epilogue

Captain's Log, 8 July, 1902
Another journey complete. The progress of science continues!

"Land ho!" Seven-year-old Aarini Szekalski twirled around the control room, her rainbow dress flaring up around her. "Home, home, home!"

Nemo smiled down at her daughter. After a month-long research voyage, it was, indeed, good to be home. As usual, they'd gathered heaps of new data. Analyzing and organizing it all would provide plenty of work during their months on land. Aleksy had papers to write and submit for publication, and Nisha had modifications to make for the experimental sensors she'd tested during the journey. Land or sea, there was always excitement to be had with this family.

"Why don't you go help Daddy move Nadia to her travel tank while I dock the ship?" Nisha suggested. "Then we'll be all ready to go the moment we arrive."

"Okay!" Aarini scampered off.

Nemo checked her watch. She'd intended to arrive in Detroit this morning, but a storm had slowed their progress by several hours. She and Aleksy still had time to make the meeting if they hurried.

The *Narwhal* glided into her permanent dock at the

marina. She'd picked up a few new dents and scrapes on their voyage and seemed eager for a rest. Nemo looked forward to shining her up and preparing her for weekend jaunts with friends and family.

A very kind soul—probably Dadi herself—had parked Nisha's new steam car near the dock. The latest design was fast, comfortable, and just the right size for two adults, a growing girl, and an axolotl.

"Are we going to Nani's house?" Aarini asked over the rush of wind as the car picked up speed.

Aleksy turned half around in his seat. "Nani's house for you and Nadia while your mother and I go to a meeting."

"Yay! I have a new drawing to show her. It has a—" Her words were cut off when another similar car flew by in the opposite direction.

Nisha leaned back in her seat, trying to hear better while keeping her eyes on the road. "A what, darling?"

"A slimy sculpin!" Aarini shouted. "I drew the insides with all the bones and guts!"

Nisha nodded. At age five, Aarini had developed a fascination with anatomical drawings, and she'd been making her own versions ever since. She particularly liked all the internal structures of animals that others often found distasteful.

"Nani said she would embroider one of my drawings onto a shawl, and I want this one," Aarini added. "I will be *beautiful*!"

Nemo couldn't hold back a bark of laughter. A fish gut shawl? How very appropriate for this family. She glanced at her husband, who was covering his own laugh with a cough.

"I hope you will always be so proud of your work, love," he said.

"I will," their daughter replied confidently. "And I will

tell Nani and Nana that I only dissect animals that have died of natural causes."

Aarini did exactly that the moment they stepped into the east parlor. Nisha's parents looked skeptical, but hugged and kissed her anyway.

Nemo's grandmother grinned broadly. "Come here and tell Boro Dadi all about it, little one."

"We must hurry to our meeting," Aleksy apologized, "but we will be back for dinner."

"I'll telephone your mother and invite her to join us," Nisha's father suggested. "She always brings her kielbasa."

"You only want the kielbasa because we are the only two non-vegetarians in the family," Nisha pointed out.

"Exactly, daughter." He slung an arm around her. "We get to eat it all!" He kissed her cheek. "Have fun with your friends, and we will see you again shortly."

Ten minutes and a dozen hugs later, Nisha and Aleksy made it out the front door. Even with the speed of the new car, they were several minutes late.

The mingled scents of tea and spirits wafted from the Mad Scientists Society alcove. The usual chairs crammed the small space, four of them occupied. Nemo and Aleksy slipped into the remaining two.

"Good afternoon." Hal lifted his teacup in greeting.

"Good—" Nemo froze, staring at her friend. His hair had been shorn to a thin layer of stubble and his eyebrows appeared... sparse. "What happened to you?"

"Ah." Hal ran a hand over his shaved head. "Slight mishap in the laboratory. Singed a bit of hair off and had to shave the rest to match."

Victor snorted. "A 'slight mishap' that made all the papers. Apparently, the flash of green light was so bright and the noise so loud that four different neighbors called the police at the same time."

Nemo chuckled. "Well, I'm sure my father was very relieved to be retired."

Hal shot Victor an annoyed look. "Victor doesn't have any right to laugh at me. How many fences did your self-driving steam car run into this week?"

"Only three." Victor straightened his shoulders as if proud of this ignoble accomplishment. "It's a vast improvement."

"As you probably remember, the sight sensors Mecha-Man uses aren't sensitive enough at the car's higher speeds," Mary explained. "But this new upgrade could be a breakthrough. We anticipate less destruction in the next round of testing."

"What did you two destroy on your latest voyage?" Victor asked.

"Nothing," Aleksy replied. "But I did learn more about the life of the *Diacyclops aleksyi*. I watched it destroy things. I have now observed it eating eleven different species of smaller zooplankton."

His smile was exactly like Aarini's had been when she'd been talking about fish guts. Even now, Nisha never failed to marvel at how her husband could enthusiastically study animals eating one another, when he refused to eat them himself. She might never understand everything about him, but he'd enriched her life and that was all that truly mattered.

She touched the submarine pendant that hung around her neck. A gift from their first wedding anniversary, made from his share of the gold. The rest he'd been doling out over the years to charitable causes, both human and animal. A fact she never hesitated to point out if he ever slipped back into his old worries about being less than worthy of this marvelous life.

"Nisha, what are your plans now?" Callie asked. She took a sip of her bright-pink cocktail. Except for the cherry at the bottom, it resembled one of Hal's experimental potions. "Will you be in town long?"

"Not if those two are going to be causing accidents." Nemo gestured at Hal and Victor.

"We will be at home until spring." Aleksy always gave the serious answer. Someone had to, Nisha supposed.

Callie beamed. "Excellent! I'm starting a new program at the library aimed at girls. Since Hal and I have four of them, I thought it would be good to give them the books and tools to pursue whatever they like in the future. I'd love it if Aarini would participate. And I was hoping you, Nisha, and Mary would join us to answer questions about being a woman scientist." Callie smiled fondly at her husband. "Our two eldest already spend hours puttering around in Hal's laboratory. Is Aarini still doing anatomical drawings?"

"Oh, yes." Nemo laughed. "If the other girls who join are anything like ours, they will want all the books, plenty of demonstrations, and hours to ask questions. Perhaps I could offer a ride on the *Narwhal* as a possible activity."

"That would be fabulous! The men can help with demonstrations and questions too, since all of us have different skills. If this goes well, perhaps next year we can run a week-long camp and have longer projects for the girls."

Victor swirled his glass of wine. "So we're plotting to train the next generation of Mad Scientists. Count me in." He held out his free hand. One-by-one, the other five stacked their hands atop his.

"In Scientific Solidarity," they said as one.

Victor raised his glass. "To friends."

Hal lifted his teacup. "To lovers," he added, giving his wife an amorous glance.

Nemo held up her whiskey flask. "To the future."

The End

About the Author

Award-winning author Catherine Stein believes that everyone deserves love and that Happily Ever After has the power to help, to heal, and to comfort. She writes sassy, sexy romance set during the Victorian and Edwardian eras. Her stories are full of action, adventure, magic, and fantastic technologies.

Catherine lives in Michigan with her husband and three rambunctious kids. She loves steampunk and Oxford commas, and can often be found dressed in Renaissance festival clothing, drinking copious amounts of tea.

Visit Catherine online at
www.catsteinbooks.com
Join her VIP mailing list for a free short story.

Instagram
@catsteinbooks

Facebook
@catsteinbooks

Also by
CATHERINE STEIN

Potions and Passions

The Earl on the Train - Book 0.5

How to Seduce a Spy - Book 1

Mishaps & Mistletoe -
A Holiday Novella -Book 1.5

Not a Mourning Person - Book 2

Once a Rake, Always a Rogue - Book 3

Love at Second Sight - Book 4

Sass and Steam

Love is in the Airship - Book 0.5

A Shot to the Heart - Book 0.75

Eden's Voice - Book 1

What Are You Doing New Year's Eve? -
A Holiday Novella - Book 1.5

Priceless - Book 2

Dead Dukes Tell No Tales - Book 3

Arcane Tales

The Scoundrel's New Con - Book 1

The Spinster's Swindle - Book 2

Mad Scientists Society

The Courtesan and Mr. Hyde - Book 1

The Electrical Affairs of Dr. Victor Franklin - Book 2

Lords of Dystopia

Earth Earls are Easy - Book 1

Other Books

Mating Habits - Book 1

Idle Nature - Book 2

My Heiress, 'Tis of Thee

Boy Meets Earl/Her Fair Lady

Available at your favorite online retailer.
www.catsteinbooks.com

Thank you so much for reading!

If you enjoyed the book and are so inclined,
I would love for you to leave a review.
Happy readers make an author's day!

I love hearing from readers, so feel free
to contact me on social media, or email:

catherine@catsteinbooks.com